DEWDROPS

DEWDROPS

Dan Flanigan

Palmetto Publishing Group
Charleston, SC

Dewdrops
Copyright © 2019 by Dan Flanigan
All rights reserved

First Edition

Printed in the United States

Paperback ISBN-13: 978-1-7336103-9-1
eBook ISBN-13: 978-1-7336103-8-4

Thanks to Thais Miller for her enthusiastic and "over the top" helpful reading, editing, commentary, and suggestions. You gave so much more than you received. You were more than a bargain—a windfall.

And to "Woman Friday" Meghan Flanigan and her miraculous ability to work with, of all people—her father—and her willingness to tackle both the difficult and the dull with enthusiasm, diligence, and competence. To my knowledge she only wept once. Meghan, the best thing in my life, ever, is that your "morning has come around."★ May it keep coming around, a day at a time, forever.

"When My Morning Comes Around," ©1996 Iris DeMent

Of course

Most of all

It's for *You*

Sparrow who fell too soon

You walked every step with me

Lived it all with me

But not to tell

TABLE OF CONTENTS

SOME COLD WAR BLUES

THE COLD HARDWOOD floor punished the boy's bony knees as he knelt beside the bed and said his morning prayers. He fingered the beads of the rosary tucked under his pillow. His Saint Christopher's medal lay cold, heavy, and hard against his thin chest. There had been a time when he had worn a scapular instead of the Saint Christopher's medal, but the square patch of sacred woolen cloth had itched too much when dry and then got too soggy with sweat and bathwater. It made him feel guilty that he could do so little when the saints, the men in the hair shirts, and the martyrs, stoned and crucified and boiled in oil and roasted over spits like barbecued chickens, had done so much. He liked to imagine the tiny bedroom as his cell, a fantasy useful for at least two of his many invented lives: monk and prisoner. Clad in long underwear, a wraith-like figure, grayish white against the whiter sheets, he slowly bowed his upper body forward until his nose touched the bed, and he remained that way for a time, bent into a rigid pose of veneration and self-denial.

"*Domine non sum dignus*," he prayed. "Lord, I am not worthy, but I ask You again to give Your grace to Mom so she will start going to church again." But then what good would it do for her to go to church if she did not divorce Ralph, his stepfather? The boy, who was called "Jack" by his friends but still "Johnnie" by the grownups, knew from his catechism classes at St. Peter's that, as a remarried divorced woman, she lived daily in mortal sin. She could not make a full and really contrite confession until she renounced Ralph altogether. Only then could she take Holy Communion without committing yet another and perhaps even more grievous offense—the taking of the Body of

Christ in the Holy Sacrament of Communion while her soul was in a state of mortal sin.

Compounding it all, Ralph was the very devil come to this world, his body tall and powerful, his heart and soul as black and stony and desiccated as cinders. So why could she not see that her soul's salvation would also bring earthly happiness both to her and her just-turned-11-year-old son? Jack worried every day that she would die in a car wreck without having made true repentance for her many sins, and without the "benefit," as the Holy Catechism said, of the Holy Sacrament of Extreme Unction and thus be cast into hell, wholly beyond her son's power to ease with his prayers her everlasting torment. And no matter how much he hated Ralph and wanted away from him—as far as he possibly could get—Jack still had to pray for Ralph too. He had to pray that he would finally be able to summon the courage to fill a pan with water and sneak up behind Ralph as the big lout dozed, as he did night after dreary night, in the Lazy-Boy recliner, and dump the pan on that beastly head while mumbling the words of the Holy Sacrament of Baptism so that even Ralph might be saved.

His upper body erect now, still kneeling, Jack reached forward, picked up his Holy Missal, and turned to the plenary indulgence prayer. Squinting his eyes in concentration, he said the prayer and released yet another anonymous soul from the searing hell-pains of Purgatory. His final prayer was for the spiritual and secular leaders of the world, especially Pope Pius and President Eisenhower.

The bedroom held a roll-away bed, a braided throw rug in the center of the room, a small "chest'er droors" as he had learned from family custom to call a chest of drawers, and an old green chair so threadbare that the stuffing shone faintly through the upholstery. He perched on the edge of the green chair and put on a black and white plaid flannel shirt, wrinkled jeans, and finally his socks—work socks, a tweedy brown with white toes and tops, like Ralph's socks.

Being Saturday, it had the prospects of being a good day. Through the still-drawn window shade he could tell it was only beginning to be light outside, the time of day that monks and prisoners arose. It should be a long time before his mother or Ralph got up. Unless Ralph had to go work overtime that day. Jack would have to be vigilantly on his guard, especially for the next hour or so, to avoid being caught in Ralph's way. What the precise consequences of such an unfortunate encounter might be, Jack could not be certain. Ralph might ignore him, order him gruffly about, or just stare at him as if he were a slug or some other detestable creature that, regrettably, had to be tolerated rather than stomped to mush.

Jack slipped out of his room and scooted quickly past the open bedroom door in which she and Ralph slept, down the short and narrow hallway, through the living room, and into the kitchen. That was all there was to the house except a bathroom, a basement, and an enclosed back porch. There was no dining room, no extra bathroom, no spare bedroom. They lived only in rented houses just large enough to contain them.

He had glimpsed them in the bed as he passed their door. They lay like lumps of dead matter, their heavy bodies saturated with beer and rapid aging. He had been too far away to smell them, but his nose had filled anyway with the memory, too often experienced, of the sickly-sweet scent of their whiskey breath. Ralph slept nearest the door, on his back, snoring, the aqua-colored blanket pulled up to his chest. His long feet—thin, delicate, and feminine—protruding out from under the blanket and dangling over the end of the bed, seemed scarcely able to support his mountainous body. The toenails were cracked, yellowing, curled, gnarled, and uncut. Fantastic, horrible things, they filled Jack with dread whenever he looked at them. He wondered if they ever gashed his mother's leg when Ralph rolled ponderously over in his sleep. Or when they f____! (his mind reeled when he mentally formed that daring, awful word Rex Jefferson, who had reached the advanced age of twelve years, had taught Jack only a month ago). How could she possibly tolerate that huge hulk of a man, who bathed only once a week and talked only in sneers, as she moaned her whimpering love for him, pitching and rolling under him like a dinghy boat on a storm-tossed sea?

Rex had called a girl a "whore." Jack asked what that word meant, and it all came out in slithering detail, malice sparkling in Rex's eyes. Many once-mysterious things had suddenly become clear. So *that* was why the nuns had made such a fuss that time he had lifted Susy Runyon's skirt. Thinking about it all, disconsolate, he concluded that this was just another of the miseries that adults inflicted on children, a companion to beer joints, cigarette smoke, domestic violence, and divorce.

He counted himself lucky that he had managed to fall asleep before they arrived home the night before. Too often he had been awake, against his will, trapped in an insomnia of dreadful anticipation and insane fascination, much the same feeling he experienced when they took him to horror movies at the drive-in. Ralph would open a beer and sit in the Lazy-Boy—their prized possession along with the exquisite china closet inherited from a long-dead aunt, an incongruity that, by comparison, exposed the drabness, the utter plainness of the rest of the furniture, an odd lot of hand-me-downs and special-sale items hawked by the braying announcers on the television—bedroom "suites" and such, paid for on installment plans that seemed to stretch out forever, certainly far beyond the lives of the house and its occupants. If Ralph could manage to guzzle his final beer of the night, strip off his work clothes, the only clothes he ever wore, and roll onto the bed and drop asleep with a terminal thud before she started in on him, they would all be spared the otherwise inevitable shouting and howling and banging session.

Ralph's hostility was boundless, a thirst never slaked. Yet these vicious combats always seemed to be provoked by her. She, who was always so neglected, dumped on, and contemptuously disregarded, would now, drunk and viper-tongued, turn on Ralph and sting him until he punched her. Since they often dragged Jack to the bars with them, where he played the pinball machine until the miasma of cigarette smoke burning his eyes drove him from the place and into the back seat of the car and fitful but still merciful sleep, he knew exactly how it would have gone. During the evening she would have built Ralph's rage step by step as she shouted, argued, and exchanged savage insults with their tavern cronies, all the time pulling and prodding at Ralph as she desperately tried to win his allegiance or at least his interest. He would either sneer at her or move to the bar to flirt with another woman. Even as far away as the pinball machine in the corner, and trying hard not even to glance their way, Jack could tell that she sensed Ralph's disgust, whether he just sat there smirking or turned his oily charm on the other woman, or, more rarely, paid her the actual attention of a vulgar direct retort. She never despaired of him. Her anger shielded her from hopelessness. Later, at home, she would bitch, nag, whine, and scream, driving Ralph into a fury, and he would, at last, pay her the very special attention of a beating, thus proving to her that she could still reach him on some level after all. Jack would cower in his room, wanting to kill Ralph but knowing his child's anger would be easily swatted aside by Ralph's massive flailing arm, leaving Jack nothing but impotent shame and irrevocable confirmation of Ralph's already infinite contempt. He had tried once to intervene but came to understand from that experience that he had only exacerbated the situation, that he had been mere mulch to feed Ralph's rage and his mother's self-pity and resentment.

"Look at you!" she would scream at Ralph. "Real tough sonuvabitch you are. Beatin' on a kid and a woman."

"Aw, shit," was all Ralph could reply, as Jack cowered there weeping, as she alternately sobbed and scolded Ralph. But then she turned on the weeping, raging boy himself and abruptly ordered him off to bed, dismissing that poor player who had lingered too long after his part was played out. He would crawl into bed and then often hear only silence. Only much later in his life would he comprehend those silences that followed those vicious ballets, silences in which the spent players groped and fondled each other in less than holy rites of false forgiveness and reconciliation.

After a few repeats of that, Jack stayed in his room, wishing he could somehow just pass through the walls of the house and fly elsewhere, forever. He had almost given up trying to rescue her from this fearsome life she had created. "I love him," she would blubber as Jack argued his case to her that she could divorce Ralph just as she had long ago, before Jack even had a memory, divorced his own father. And he had begun then to understand, almost unconsciously, that he must learn to protect himself from both of them. He wanted to run away, but he was afraid he would falter and fail a day or two out on the road and have to slink back, head bowed and eyes downcast, to an even more shamed existence.

In the kitchen on this early Saturday morning there remained only the strewn detritus of Friday night: five empty beer bottles, two full and reeking ashtrays, the popcorn pan on the front burner of the stove, the popcorn bowl empty save for a few old maids stuck in a hardened puddle of congealed grease on the bottom. The kitchen smelled of fishsticks, popcorn, cigarette butts, and flat beer.

Jack pulled down on the window shade, worried that he would lose his grip and the shade would leap up with a loud flap and wake his mother and Ralph. But the ascent was altogether smooth. And—Surprise! His breath skipped, his eyes bulged. Snow. Snow everywhere. The first big snowfall of the winter covered everything. He wondered if the other boys would be out yet. He rushed to the front door that opened onto the uncovered front porch on which the snow had drifted at last a foot high. No one was out yet. Smoke trickled from a few chimneys. The other kids were probably watching cartoons. He suddenly wished they lived in the country again where he could go tramping in the snowy woods with his dog, Duke, and walk along on the ice of the creeks, as alone and serene as Daniel Boone himself in uninhabited territory. Back then he had lived the imagined life of a woodsman, just him and Duke in a cabin in the forest, going to town once a month for supplies, hunting and trapping most of their food. But Ralph would not let him have even a BB gun, and Duke had chased one car too many. Jack had watched the old couple in the car that killed Duke proceed on slowly, blithely down the road as if they had not just crushed the entrails out of the only worthwhile thing in Jack's life. Ralph had dug a meager hole and pitched Duke in. Duke hit the bottom with a muffled thud, and Jack could only stand and weep and watch Ralph throw dirt on the dear dead dog. He wished that dogs could go to heaven too and wondered for the first time whether God really was All-Just as the Holy Catechism claimed Him to be.

Woodsmen ate hearty breakfasts: thick slabs of bacon, pancakes, eggs, coffee. Jack had cooked pancakes once, and even eaten them, though they were raw in the middle and burnt on the outside. He had no use at all for eggs. Who in the world thought up the idea of eating the eggs of *chickens* anyway, to say nothing of drinking the milk of *cows*? In the refrigerator this morning he found a plastic package of thin, droopy, gelatinous strips of bacon and in the freezer a box of pre-sliced French toast that only had to be warmed in the oven before eating. A black, pot-bellied stove would be best for woodsman fare, but the gas range would have to suffice.

The instructions on the French toast box told him to pre-heat the oven to 425 degrees. He grabbed a box of wooden matches, opened the oven door, and located the hole for the pilot light. He struck the tiny match—which burned way too fast—turned the knob with his left hand to 425, bent over the little hole at the front of the oven, and very quickly—for now the match was burning his fingertips—touched the match to the hole.

Later he vividly recalled a dim flash and a *Whoosh* that knocked him backward. He was afraid to scream. Thinking he had been struck blind and that his face might have caught fire, he began to cry. He opened his eyes very slowly and thanked God he could still see. A mirror. He had to find a mirror. The only mirror he could think of was the one on the front of the medicine cabinet in the bathroom next to their bedroom. He crept up the stairs to the bathroom, expecting to find in the mirror a visage right out of the horror films—blackened, blistered, dripping goo. But his skin was not burnt, though his eyebrows looked odd, and when he touched his forehead, hair from his bangs fell out into the sink. Sneaking back downstairs again, he found the kitchen full of gas fumes. He rushed to turn off the stove and opened the door to the drafty, unheated back porch to let the gas smell escape.

He settled for plain toast and cold cereal and watched cartoons. It had once thrilled him to watch Pinky Lee come careening down his little slippery slide at the beginning of the show, but he was tiring of Pinky's nonsense. The Andy Devine show, stories of turbaned Indian boys riding elephants, bored him except for Froggy plunking his magic twanger and croaking "Hi-ya, kids, Hi-ya, hi-ya." Jack wondered if they had cartoons in Russia. He often imagined himself as a revolutionary leader there, fighting a guerilla war with only a handful of followers, sometimes eluding the government in the frozen wasteland of the steppes, sometimes huddling over a forbidden radio in a basement room in one of the vast gray cities. The government tried to deny his existence, but he had become a legend among the people. Sometimes they captured and imprisoned him, but he always managed to escape just before they marched him blindfolded before the firing squad.

Suddenly Ralph was upon him! In his baggy boxer shorts and sleeveless undershirt and moving as fast as he had ever seen Ralph move. "Jesus Christ," Ralph muttered, not looking at Jack, heading toward the kitchen. Jack's heart began to pound. Ralph must have smelled the gas! He heard the back porch door slam shut. Ralph came to the doorway between the kitchen and the living room, his eyes flickering and dancing in anger, his neck distended like a cobra about to strike. "Didn't ya know the God-damn door was open? Too lazy ta get your ass up and close it." Jack said nothing. Ralph snorted, waved his hand at Jack as if pushing him away and went back into the kitchen. Jack thanked the Lord that Ralph had not smelled the gas.

Ralph made coffee amidst mumbled imprecations. "Bitch...Lazier'n hell...Won't get up off her ass ta fix breakfast..." Soon the coffee was perking and Ralph was stomping back up the stairs to the bedroom. "Why won't you get up off your lazy ass and fix breakfast?"

Jack heard her say "I'll be happy to, honey. Wha'dya want?"

"Forget it. It's too late now."

"I'll be happy to."

"Forget it."

A few minutes later Ralph returned downstairs in his work clothes and black engineer boots. Jack heard him dial the telephone in the kitchen and tell someone to meet him somewhere. Ralph paced back and forth across the kitchen doorway, listening to someone on the other end of the line and staring at Jack. At first Jack tried to avert his eyes, but after a while he stared back with a stricken deer-in-the-headlights sort of look.

"What're you lookin' at?" Ralph said.

"Nothin'," Jack said.

Jack could not decide whether to remain there or try to escape to the bedroom, or to the basement to his dartboard for the world dart tossing championships, or to the plastic army helmet hanging from a hook suspended from the low basement ceiling, a makeshift miniature basketball goal. He would jump and whirl and shoot and hook and dunk a rolled-up pair of socks bound with rubber bands into the helmet for hours, playing the entire semifinals of the NCAA tourney, or the NBA championship, or, most fun of all, the All-Star game.

Ralph hung up the phone and walked through the living room toward the front door, favoring Jack with a contemptuous sideways glance on his way through. Ralph was searching for the newspaper, the only evidence Jack had ever seen that Ralph was literate. If Ralph got absorbed in the newspaper, it could mean another interminable hour of his menacing company.

"Well, where's the God-damn paper?" he heard Ralph ask the silent, frozen world.

Ralph poked his head back inside.

"Get down the basement and get the God-damn shovel."

Jack retrieved the shovel from the dusty basement and handed it to Ralph, who was standing on the porch in the cold without even shivering. Ralph took a few swipes and sweeps with the shovel but failed to uncover the newspaper. "Shit," Ralph said as he surrendered, leaning the shovel against the banister on the porch. Jack moved well back into the room to make way for Ralph who came in stomping snow all over the rug.

"I want you to shovel the porch and the walk," Ralph said.

"Okay."

Jack went back to his chair to finish watching the cartoons.

"*Now.* Get your lazy ass movin'."

"Can't I finish watchin'?"

"Now." Ralph stepped toward him, threatening—but for some unfathomable reason Ralph hardly ever hit him, only that one time when he had grabbed Jack by the arm and, using only one hand, lifted the boy up in the air like he would lift a chicken to wring its neck, and pounded Jack in the ass with the flat of his heavy paw as Jack struggled and twisted, too terrified to scream or even cry.

JACK SHOVELED, CURSING under his breath. He had regular chores and innumerable irregular ones as well. They always had surprises for him, new things to do—shoveling snow, hosing down and sweeping the basement, washing and waxing the floors, and on and on. This must have been just like Cinderella felt, he would often think as he struggled to complete some irritating task. It seemed he only managed to do what his mother called "a half-assed job." He sometimes felt guilty for being resentful because he knew that monks labored uncomplainingly at much harder chores than his own, but he also knew that his school friends did not have to do such things, and his relative deprivation fueled his resentment, which then fed his guilt, all of it combining to produce what Ralph called "a piss-poor job" at almost every task they assigned him.

By the time Ralph came out to go to work, Jack had cleared a path on the porch and raked over the front steps and started on the front walkway. It was another of his piss-poor jobs. Ralph surveyed it with disdain. The path Jack had carved was much narrower than the sidewalk itself, and he had not scraped all the way down to the concrete, leaving a rough and slippery mat of snow and ice.

"Gimme that," Ralph said, grabbed the shovel and began to blaze a trail down the sidewalk to his car, which was parked on the street in front of the house. Jack stood on the front steps and dismally compared his life-and-death struggles to Ralph's effortless rhythm and easy power, and he wondered if he would ever amount to anything in life.

Soon Ralph was standing at the front curb holding the shovel out to him. "Com'ere and get the God-damn thing. Why can't you do anything right?"

Jack took the shovel and began to frantically dig out the sides of the path that Ralph had started. For a few strokes he seemed to have the hang of it, but he soon lapsed into desperate and half-hearted combat. The car's engine chugged then died. Jack prayed that it would start. If it did not start, Jack would have to endure another eternity of anxiety while Ralph waited for a jump start or a ride. But Ralph held magical sway over mechanical things, and the engine soon rumbled into life. He then scraped the ice off the windows and drove away.

"Fuck you," muttered Jack—a new phrase Rex had taught him—as Ralph drove out of sight, but he kept on working for a few minutes in case Ralph circled the block and came around to check on him. Once sure that Ralph would not return, he grabbed the shovel handle with both hands and flung it as far as he could. It sailed ten yards or so before it plunged into the snow and disappeared into the front yard. He looked around to see if anyone was watching. Nobody. He was clear.

He trudged around the side of the house, his galoshes squeaking in the snow, his boot prints marring the perfect placid smoothness of the drifts. The house was in a two or three-block enclave, less prosperous than the surrounding neighborhood, with a scruffy semi-rural quality about it though it was located near the very center of the town. There was nothing in the backyard except a clothesline and a trash barrel at the back edge of the yard next to the alley. His house sat in the middle of an uphill street, the fourth one down from the top of the hill. The Kryzanowskis lived next door up the hill and, next to them, the MacDonalds. A fieldstone wall, five feet high, separated the Kryzanowskis' yard from the MacDonalds' yard. The MacDonalds were an old couple who yelled at kids that strayed into their yard, but Mr. MacDonald was retired, and the bickering old man and woman had piled into their ancient rusty camper and gone away to somewhere warm for the winter. The Hartigans lived above the MacDonalds, on the corner at the top of the hill. The little Hartigan kids, lumbering around awkwardly in their snowsuits, were trying to build a snowman in their backyard. They looked like penguins as they waddled stiff-legged through the snow, their excitement expressing itself in occasional cries of delight.

Jack wondered if he should drag his sled out of the basement and try to sled down the alley. If he ventured back into the house, he might encounter his mother and be saddled with any number of chores. He determined to let fate decide. If the outside door to the basement was open, he would get the sled; if not, he would do something else. He tugged the screen door open, dragging it through the drifted snow. And Bingo!—the inner door was unlocked.

Pulling his sled behind him, Jack slogged up the alley, the sled rope freezing rapidly in his hand. His cloth mittens were already sopping wet. Soon they would be frozen clumps. By the time he reached the top of the alley, he had figured out that sledding was a bad idea. On the day of a snowfall the snow was usually too deep and too loose for sledding. He tried it anyway and slid only about three yards before he crunched to a halt. So frustrating. Snow covered the front of his sled and his face. For a moment he wished he could just stay there in the snow, maybe just go to sleep and die right there and pass on up to Heaven. But, instead, he stood up and wondered what to do next.

A snowball slammed against his upper back. Enraged, he turned around, ready to fight, but it was only Andy Maher, who was aiming yet another snowball, at Jack's head this time. Andy missed with the snowball and charged and tackled Jack before Jack could make his own snowball to return fire. "Okay, say uncle," demanded Andy, who was bigger and tougher and had Jack hopelessly pinned. "And promise you won't hit me with a snowball."

"Okay, I promise."

Andy let him up.

"Didn' say uncle!" he cried as he tackled Andy.

They wrestled until Andy again had Jack decisively pinned.

"Okay," Jack said, "I give up."

"No. Say uncle, you fink."

"Uncle."

Andy let him up again, and he brushed the snow from his clothes.

"Now I'll hafta go in an' change," Jack said.

"Why?"

"'Cause I'm all wet now, ya dumb cluck."

"No, you don't. Let's go get Peter. You can dry off at his house."

PETER SWANSON AND his little sisters—five-year-old twins— all of them still in their pajamas, were watching *Captain Midnight*. Jack did not care much for *Captain Midnight*. He had once persuaded his mother to buy *Ovaltine*, the product sponsor of the show. It gagged him, but Ralph said he had to drink it until it was gone. So he drank another glass right in front of them both, then went into the bathroom and stuck his fingers down his throat and threw up loudly enough for them to hear him. The *Ovaltine* sat in the cupboard day after day for more than a month. During the first week he woke in terror each morning, sure that Ralph waited for him downstairs with glass, spoon, and *Ovaltine* in hand. After the first week he was able to put it out of his mind most of the time. Finally, one day he opened the cupboard and the *Ovaltine* was gone. He sent a special prayer to heaven for this miracle, which he suspected had been engineered by his mother who did often try to protect him from Ralph, at considerable risk to her own well-being.

"Let's go outside," Andy said, restless as always.

"I wanna watch *Sky King*," Peter said, and the twins clapped with glee.

Jack's heart sank, for he found only a yawning emptiness in the adventures of the crew-cut middle-aged pilot who wore the dumbest-looking cowboy hat Jack had ever seen. Even Sky's young niece, Penny, left him cold, a dip of a girl if ever there was one.

"Come on," Andy said. "It's a snow day."

"All right," Peter said.

The twins begged Peter to stay with them, which only sealed his resolve to depart, for he could not be thought to want to do what the little kids wanted. Andy and Jack followed Peter into a neat and sunny kitchen full of wafting baking smells. Peter's mother and father sat at a small table in the breakfast nook drinking coffee and poring over some sheets of paper with numbers written on them.

"Hi, boys," Mr. Swanson said.

"Hi," they replied.

"I bet you boys would like some coffee cake," Mrs. Swanson said.

Andy and Jack had been hoping for this since they had entered the house. Indeed, this was an unspoken but vital reason why they had undertaken the two-block pilgrimage to Peter's house in the first place.

"I'll get ready," Peter said and climbed the narrow back stairs to his room, which had once been a maid's quarters. The Swansons brushed their papers aside, and the boys sat down at the kitchen table and ate the coffee cake and drank the milk that Mrs. Swanson served them.

"Why da they call it coffee cake?" Andy asked. "Is there coffee in it?"

The Swansons laughed and told him it was made to go with coffee.

"I like it better with milk," Andy said in solemn judgment, and the Swansons laughed again.

The Swansons asked about Andy's parents and Jack's mother. They then cautiously inquired if Jack had seen his father—meaning his real father—lately, and he said, "Not since last year."

After a brief, embarrassed silence, Mr. Swanson said, "Well, boys, next year at this time we'll be playing basketball." Mr. Swanson would coach the team, Peter's team, just as he had already coached the kids' youth baseball teams and would next year coach their football team as well.

As the boys buttoned up to go outside, Jack reflected enviously upon Peter's life—a comfortable house, nice parents who didn't hate each other, best of all a real father who actually liked his son, hardly any chores at all, weekends at the lakes and summer vacations in some wonderland up North, homemade coffee cake two or three times a week—so often you just took it for granted—and little twin sisters to boss around, wrestle with, and scare the daylights out of as they scurried unsuspectingly around a dark corner of the house.

OUTSIDE, WALKING UP the street, the boys debated what to do.

"How 'bout a snowman?" Andy said.

"No fun," Peter said. "Kid stuff."

"Then let's go up ta the hospital roof an' throw snowballs at cars."

Peter silently weighed the pleasures of such a dangerous adventure against the possibility of apprehension and punishment.

"How 'bout this," Peter said. "Let's find a good place an' build a snow fort an' have a snowball war."

"Who with?" Jack said.

"I don' know. We'll find somebody."

"Where?"

"The MacDonalds," Andy said. "They're gone for the winter. We'll attack the sledders when they come down the alley."

"Nobody'll sled today," Jack said. "The snow's not right."

But Peter had grander visions. "Yeah, the MacDonalds," he said. "They won't be back until summer. Maybe we can have the same fort all winter. It'll be like a clubhouse, with dues and a password."

"At least until it melts," Jack said, nervously correcting their leader a second time.

So they followed Peter, as they almost always did. Peter picked and chose for them from the fads raging in the outside world—hula hoops, coonskin caps, bubble blowing, whiffle ball—the ones worthy of their allegiance. Peter established their morality, their aspirations, their fears and hopes for the future. He would lead them on shoplifting expeditions, then decide that they must return the goods or their money's worth so they would be fully cleansed of the sin of theft. And they always did what he so enthusiastically advocated, sneaking twenty-three cents or seventy-eight cents—always the exact amount of the stolen item with estimated sales tax too—onto the rim of a cash register in a department store, often a greater risk than stealing the stuff in the first place. Peter would decide which colleges they would attend and which sports they would choose for their professional careers, for there was no doubt in any of their minds that they would remain together forever.

Jack's cloth mittens were thoroughly frozen now. His hands were stumps of cold. His jeans were wet, and his legs, especially the soft flesh of his inner thighs, chafed and stung. He tried to balance in his mind his physical discomfort against the peril of going back into the house to change, and he knew that both the peril and discomfort would increase as the morning progressed. At least he needed to get a dry pair of mittens. Besides, he had forgotten to use the Swansons' bathroom and was about to wet his pants.

"I gotta take a pee," he said. "You guys wanna come in a minute?" He hoped their presence would keep his mother and her list of chores at bay.

"Naw," Peter said. "Go on. We'll start on the fort."

Carefully picking his way up the icy front walk, Jack wondered if he would have to finish shoveling it. Maybe Ralph would not come home at all that day. Ralph might just call his mother and tell her to meet him at the beer joint. Or maybe there would be another snowfall to cover Jack's procrastination. Or maybe Ralph would just forget about it as he had forgotten about the *Ovaltine*. Jack plunged into the yard and retrieved the shovel. No use forgetting about it later and having to explain to Ralph why it was buried in the snow in the middle of the yard.

His mother was not awake. He played like the stealthy Russian revolutionary and wished the floorboards and his dripping galoshes would not squeak so much. He sat down on the toilet to pee to make less noise. He decided not to flush it. She was buried in the covers, lying on her stomach, only her foot dangling out. Deciding not to risk the time and noise it would take to change his clothes, he put the wet mittens on the radiator to dry and sneaked his other pair from the chest of drawers in his room, then dashed down the hall and the stairs, onto the back porch, and out the back door. He tried to forget the chafing and burning on his legs and that his neck was sweaty and his stocking hat dripping wet because the snow caked on it had melted in the warm house.

He walked across his own yard and the Kryzanowskis' and climbed the chest-high fieldstone wall that separated the Kryzanowskis from the

MacDonalds. Peter and Andy had already made great progress on the fort. They had completed a low parapet, six feet wide, a foot tall and growing. They had situated the fort close to the alley in a small clearing between a massive oak tree and a huge propane tank that they sometimes pretended was an atom bomb planted there by Russian saboteurs.

Peter ordered Andy to begin making snowballs while he and Jack worked on the fort. "Ammunition," Peter said.

They fell into an easy and efficient rhythm, forgetting about the cold, saying little, concentrating on the work. Within half an hour the parapet had grown to four feet in height, and Andy had stacked up forty-seven hard-packed snowballs. Jack looked up and saw the Gorski brothers standing in their backyard across the alley.

"Whatcha doin'?" Tom Gorski said.

"What's it look like?" Andy sarcastically replied. "It's a fort."

Andy threw a snowball that whizzed over the Gorskis' ducking heads. The Gorskis conferred, then Tom Gorski went running off, and his brother Mike started making snowballs.

"Looks like we're gonna have our war," Peter said. "I'm gonna go get Larry. Andy, you go get Big Bob. Jack, why don't ya start on the side walls? We'll make it a three-sided fort."

Like World War I combatants during a temporary truce, the alley a strip of no-mans-land between them, Jack on his side, and Mike Gorski on his, each worked silently and feverishly making snowballs. Jack thought a couple of times about flinging a snowball at Mike, and he was sure that Mike was thinking the same thing. But each of them honored the unspoken truce. Tom Gorski returned with Tim Dietrich and another boy, a very big boy that Jack did not recognize. Must be a public school kid, he thought.

"Where's your buddies?" Tim Dietrich shouted over at him.

"They'll be back in a minute," Jack said, eyeing the pile of snowballs Andy had made, worrying that the four boys across the alley would decide to jump him while he was alone. Yet he found himself almost welcoming the idea, unconsciously reveling in the underdog role.

"Maybe we oughtta just come on over there and knock down your fort and steal all your snowballs," Tom Gorski said.

"No fair," Jack said. "Four against one."

"So what?" said the big kid that Jack didn't know.

Yeah, Jack thought, disgusted. He was a public school kid all right.

"Jack's right," said Mike Gorski. "Four against one ain't fair."

Mike's a good guy, Jack thought. Not like that brother of his. Peter came back with Larry Zarda. Andy came back without Big Bob.

"Look at how big that guy is," Peter said, eyeing the public school kid.

Peter looked around at Andy. "Is Big Bob comin'?" Peter asked.

Andy shook his head no, looking glum and a little ashamed. "He says he's too old for this stuff."

They all shuddered a little. They always won when Big Bob joined their side. But Big Bob had abandoned them now, grown up all of a sudden, passed on to a different world and left them behind.

"Well, we better get goin'," Jack said.

The opposing sides worked feverishly to finish their forts. Since Jack's group had a head start, they finished theirs first.

"Okay," Peter said, "everybody start makin' snowballs now."

But Andy was restless, itching for the fight to start.

"We better attack 'em before they get ready," Andy said. "A surprise attack."

Before Peter could rein him in, Andy grabbed three snowballs, dashed across the alley and heaved two of the snowballs at the opposing fort.

"Hey!" someone yelled from behind the opposing fort, and Andy was peppered with snowballs as he pitched his last one and scampered back across the alley.

"Jeez," Andy said. "They got six guys over there now. Davis 'n Lopinski are over there too."

"We need a flag of truce," Peter said. None being available, he yelled, "Hey, no fair! You got more guys than us!"

"So what?" The public school kid again.

"And you're bigger," Peter said. As usual he had honed in on his adversaries' vulnerability, in this case their sense of fair play (all but the public school kid's anyway). The enemy troops huddled, deliberating, then sent Ed Lopinski over—the smallest, most awkward, most disliked kid in the neighborhood.

"Come on, Lopinski," Andy said in disgust.

"We'll take turns makin' ammunition," Peter said. "Three defenders and two makin' snowballs. Jack, you and Lopinski make the ammunition first."

Jack worked sullenly beside Lopinski as Andy, Larry, and Peter exchanged snowball cannonades with the opposing fort amidst laughter and merry shouting. He hated Peter just then. Sticking him with Lopinski like that. But he would show Peter. He would show them all if given half a chance. And why should he do what Peter told him to do anyway? For some reason he didn't understand, he was suddenly thinking about Ralph, thinking about Ralph standing there at the curb holding the shovel out to him and saying, "Com'ere and get the God-damn thing. Why can't you do anything right?"

Disregarding Peter's orders, Jack grabbed some snowballs. His first shot almost knocked Mike Gorski's stocking hat off.

"Hey, you're supposed to stay here with me," Lopinski whined.

"Yeah, Jack," Peter said.

Jack said nothing but kept defiantly flinging snowballs across the alley.

"Okay, Jack," Peter said ominously.

Jack acted as if he hadn't heard. So let Peter try to punish him somehow, maybe get the other boys to give Jack the "silent treatment" for a week or so, make Jack so miserable he wanted to die, then suddenly befriend him again. Well, let him then, Jack thought. Just let him.

The battle ebbed and flowed for a quarter of an hour. Each side took care to keep replenishing its ammunition. On Jack's side of the alley a rough democracy prevailed as each boy automatically began to take his turn away from the fray to make new snowballs. Even Peter took his turn, and Jack felt as though he had won a small victory. Each side occasionally sent out raiding parties. Andy charged the enemy fort alone and returned with a nasty red mark on his cheek. A band of enemy raiders flanked around by the fieldstone wall, using it for cover, but they were bombarded and driven off when they tried to climb over it.

Jack did not join the raiding parties. He stood straight up, several feet back from the parapet, exposed to enemy fire but confident of his ability to dodge and duck, waited for an opponent to rise from cover, then threw at him with all his might. He calculated he was batting about six-hundred, better than anyone else on either side.

Frankie Ryan showed up. Andy, who lived next door to Frankie and bullied him mercilessly, told Frankie he couldn't play, that he would make the sides uneven. "You're a crybaby anyway," he said. But Peter, unable to pass up the chance of grabbing an advantage, allowed Frankie to at least make ammunition for them, though he would be forbidden to throw any snowballs. And Frankie was happy to do what Peter said, glad to be admitted to the group in even the most servile role.

Jack was disgusted. "That ain't right, Peter," he said with clenched teeth. "We got one more guy now."

"Yeah," Lopinksi said, "you got one more guy now. That's no fair."

Lopinski rushed to the snowball pile, knocked Frankie Ryan down, smashed as many snowballs as he could and skittered across the alley toward the other fort.

"Traitor!" Andy yelled at Lopinksi.

Lopinksi stopped in the middle of the alley and turned to throw a snowball at Andy when Peter caught him full in the face with a hard-thrown snowball and knocked him down. Snowballs pounded the fallen boy. Andy rushed him, rubbed his face in the snow, and kicked him in the side for good measure. Cries of "Traitor!" filled the air. The combatants in the Gorski fort, perhaps not fully understanding Lopinski's intent, failed to come to his aid. Nobody liked Lopinski. After Andy let him up, he hobbled off toward home, crying and utterly defeated.

There was a lull in the battle. Both sides stopped to rest and replenish their ammunition. Jack noticed that Peter was not speaking to him. The silent treatment had begun. Jack thought for a minute about picking a fight with his own side. Why not a three-sided war? Him against all the rest of them on both sides. But he quickly decided that was a bad idea. He had no ammunition of his own. He wouldn't last more than a minute or two alone against all of them. He moved away from Peter and looked around the side of the fort across the alley. When he saw what was on the other side, his stomach churned.

"Hoods," he said, the word almost catching in his throat.

"What?" Peter said.

"Hoods."

"Oh, shit," Peter said.

Tim Dietrich and the public school kid had left, and three strangers had imposed themselves on the opposing fort. Perhaps they had been walking down the street looking for trouble as always, seen the war in progress at the back of the Gorskis' house and became the Gorskis' unwelcome allies. They were big and mean-looking boys on their way to becoming what the neighborhood kids called "hoods" and the newspapers called "juvenile delinquents," thugs who would swagger down the street and chortle with malice as they watched a group of playing kids a block away see them coming and scatter like scared rabbits. They were older than the other boys. They did not wear galoshes. They did not even wear gloves. Their leader had a bullet head, and one of his buck teeth was chipped off at the end.

Jack, Andy, Peter, Larry, and Frankie Ryan (who hardly counted) were arrayed against the Gorskis, Mike Davis, and the three hoods. Six to five. Really six to four since Frankie was almost useless. When Peter rose to cry "No fair!" he was blasted with snowballs. "It's the Alamo," Peter said. Jack remembered that every man in the Alamo had been killed and was amazed that he still was not afraid.

The snow was getting icier, harder. The sky was darker. It looked like it might snow again soon. They heard Andy's mother screeching, calling him home. She would be standing on the front porch, indignant as always, her eyes bright with purpose, like a chicken bawking at an intruder in the barnyard. She was the only fear Andy knew.

"Sorry, guys," Andy said, "I gotta go."

When he jumped up to run home, he was bombarded with snowballs.

"Wait up," Larry Zarda said. He looked back guiltily at Peter and Jack. "Geez, guys," he said, "it's probably lunchtime. I gotta be home for lunch. Maybe we better retreat."

Jack watched Peter's fear struggle with his image of himself as one of the glorious Alamo heroes. "No," Peter said, "We'll stay. We'll make 'em think you're runnin' for help. Run off in different directions."

Larry and Andy scooted on their way. "Tell Big Bob ta hurry!" Peter yelled after the running boys. Jack understood that tactic. Peter hoped the Gorskis would think Big Bob was coming and tell the hoods just who Big Bob was. Big Bob could make mincemeat out of all three of those hoods single-handed. And Jack had a sudden crazy hope that Big Bob would any second come loping around the corner of Jack's house down there below the fieldstone wall, like the cavalry coming to save the wagon train.

Frankie Ryan stayed with Jack and Peter, trying to prove that Andy was wrong about him, feebly lobbing snowballs over the parapet from a sitting position. "Stop it," Peter ordered Frankie. "You're just wastin' ammunition." Frankie jumped up to prove his mettle and got hit in the eye. He didn't seem to have the sense to duck back down. Snowballs rained down on him. Soon he was wailing and utterly defenseless. A snowball smacked into the side of his face. He cried even harder.

"I'm gonna tell," Frankie wailed at Peter.

"We didn't do nothin'," Peter said.

Peter and Jack watched Frankie shuffle off toward home, proving that Andy was right about him after all. Every few steps a snowball hit him in the back or head. The hoods kept taunting him, calling him a "pussy." The way they said "pussy" made Jack shudder, and he guessed that Peter was feeling the same way though Peter would never admit it.

Jack inched his head around the side of the fort and looked across the alley. Mike Davis was gone. He had probably waited until the hoods were preoccupied to their front, then, saying nothing, hightailed it, putting all the distance he could between himself and such bad company. These were the type of guys your mother always told you never to play with or remain in their company for even an instant. Mike Gorski had also slipped away. It was Peter and Jack against the three hoods and Tom Gorski, and Tom was almost a hood himself.

Peter took a stick and poked two eyeholes in the front wall so he and Jack could lie on their stomachs and see in front of them. Jack wondered whether the Alamo heroes had looked out like that at Santa Ana's hordes.

"I'm cold," Peter said.

Jack was cold too. His clothes were clotted with snow turning to ice. He was wet all over, especially his stocking hat and mittens.

"I gotta get home," Peter said. "Come on."

Jack said nothing, but there was no hesitation in him. He wasn't going home. He was going to stay in the fort until they drove him out or gave up trying. He groped for a way to spare Peter's feelings. Jack knew that Peter would never forgive him for being braver.

"Come on," Peter said again. "There's more'a them an' they're bigger."

"You go first," Jack said. "I'll cover ya and run on home right after ya. But don't let 'em see ya leave."

Peter considered Jack's proposal for a few moments, no doubt making sure it left him able to flee with his honor intact.

"Okay," he said finally.

They heard Tom Gorski across the alley. "Hey, pussies. Stand up 'n fight."

Jack turned to Peter and said, "One more battle before ya go," then he and Peter jumped up and fired round after round, throwing and ducking, bending down to get more snowballs from the dwindling pile, throwing and ducking again.

"Make some more for me, will ya?" Jack said, and Peter complied, and for the first time that day Jack was the leader, which nearly always happened when he and Peter were alone but almost never when they were in a group. As Peter knelt down to make more snowballs, Jack exchanged fire with Gorski and the hoods. A snowball hit him in the forehead, leaving a sear of pain, maybe a gash too. There had been a rock in that snowball. He was afraid, but he said nothing to Peter.

"That oughtta be enough, ought'nt it?" Peter said.

"That's great," Jack said. "Okay. Go behind the tank an' up the terrace through the Hartigans' yard. I don't think they'll see ya leave that way."

"See ya later," Peter said and crawled on his hands and knees around the tank.

Jack looked through one of the eyeholes that Peter had made. The hoods and Tom Gorski were conferring about something. Jack was a bit afraid, but he felt a strange fascination. He thought, yes, this was the way it should be, him alone against the other four, just like in the game they played on summer nights that they called "Left Foot Right". One of them would hide his eyes and count fast to fifty while the others fanned out. They played within carefully defined boundaries over an area of two or three blocks. The kid who was "it," the one hiding his eyes, would yell "Fifty!" and come hunting for the others. He would chase down and tag another player, who then joined his captor in the hunt, until, one by one, the hunter group got larger and larger and there remained only one of them, one boy hiding and running from the others. Jack was usually the last to be caught. There had been no greater thrill for him in life than being the last of the runners, alone against them all, outrunning and outwitting them. He was a fast runner and a desperate boy, so it was always very hard for them to run him down, and sometimes they grew angry and handled him roughly when they caught him.

Jack failed to see Tom Gorski leave his fort and circle down behind the fieldstone wall, but he caught Tom climbing up the wall and drove Tom away while the hoods blasted away at him, hitting him with half a dozen snowballs. He turned and fought them furiously, alternately firing at the hoods and then at Tom as Tom ran back to the fort. But Tom knew now that Jack was alone, which he would report to the hoods. It was only a matter of time before they would charge him.

He knew he should go on home right now, but he did not want to go home, did not want to spend an endless afternoon in the house doing chores or watching television with his mother, waiting with dread for Ralph to come home, watching cowboy movies where the same old cowboy jumped off the same old rock onto the unsuspecting horseman below. More than anything, he wanted to stay right there, in the fort, no matter how cold it got. If only they would not charge him. If only they would just give him up for dead. Or maybe Big Bob would happen to come by to help him. But he saw through the eyehole that the hoods and Gorski were talking, and Gorski was surely telling them that Jack was alone. Right now none of them was paying any attention to him. He leaped up with two snowballs. They had only begun to react to his movement in their peripheral vision when he caught the chipped-tooth bullet-headed hood on the side of the head with one snowball and Gorski full in the face with the other.

The hood grabbed the side of his face, bent over for a moment, then looked up and across the alley at Jack. "Motherfucker!" the hood yelled and led the others in a headlong rush across the alley at Jack, who backed across the MacDonalds' yard toward his house, throwing as he retreated.

Gorski and the hoods plowed through the front of the fort, kicked and stomped it into powder and clumps, grabbed as many snowballs as they could carry, then turned to deal with Jack, who was still moving backward toward the edge of the MacDonalds' yard.

Misjudging where he was, Jack fell backward off the fieldstone wall that separated the MacDonalds' yard from the Kryzanowskis' and landed flat on his back. The fall knocked him breathless. He floundered helplessly in the snow like a turtle flipped over on its back. The hoods and Tom Gorski stood at the top of the wall hurling snowballs down on him. The snowballs were icy. Some had rocks in them. Several hit Jack in the face before he could gather his senses enough to cover his face with his arms. He heard one of them say, "Let's just beat the fucker up." His porch seemed too far away ever to reach. He wondered if this was how Saint Stephen, the first martyr, had swooned when the mob stoned him to death. Somehow he was able to roll over and lurch to his knees. He heard a thud as one of them jumped down off the wall. If they ever got him down, they might never let him up. He leaped up and began to run, and the hoods jumped down off the wall and pursued him like baying hounds chasing a frenzied hare. Tom Gorski stayed on top of the wall, and when he saw what was happening in Jack's backyard, he ran home as fast as he could and watched the rest from his kitchen window.

Jack fell as he reached the back stairs to his house. He started crawling up the stairs. A sharp, hard-thrown rock gashed the back of his head. He wondered if he had lost his stocking hat. It was the only one he owned. His mother would be mad at him for losing his only stocking hat. A ball of ice speared him in his hand as he reached for the knob to pull the screen door open. He managed to open the screen door and then the inner door and dive into the enclosed back porch. But before he could close the door, a huge clump of ice bounced off the door, hit him in the face and crashed into the porch, scattering in chunks all over the floor. He slammed the door to the outside shut and bolted it. The doorknob turned furiously. The door banged against the bolt. They were trying to come in after him.

Several cars had driven through the alley during the morning, and their tires had churned up slabs of hard-packed snow. A row of large icicles hung from the Kryzanowskis' garage. The hoods broke off the icicles and gathered some of the slabs of snow. He heard them shout, "Come on out, ya little pussy! Ya chickenshit, come out. Come on out, chickenshit."

Jack crouched in a corner, flinching as the brittle icicles crashed and the slabs of snow pounded against the back door. A window shattered. He wondered if they would tear the very house down to get at him. His nose was bleeding all over his only coat. Then he heard another kind of thud, a pounding, coming from the inside of the house.

"God-damn it!" he heard her yell. "What's goin' on?"

She came stomping out into the porch from the kitchen. She had just gotten up out of bed, perhaps only after the icicles and the slabs of snow exploding against the house had roused her. She had not even put on a robe over her shorty pajamas. The broken purple veins in her thighs pulsed madly. Her breasts flopped as she stepped.

"Do you know those boys? Did you do something to 'em?" she screamed at him.

She was squinting out the shattered window. She could hardly see without her glasses.

"Well?" she demanded and turned on him as if she would hit him. She had not bothered to put in her false teeth. She seemed like a monstrous avenging angel.

"Well? What have you done?" she demanded again. But he could not muster a word, not utter a sound. Then she saw that his nose was bleeding. Her angry eyes seemed to bulge, and she turned back to the shattered window. "You boys go home!" she screamed as Jack wondered how he had brought this terrible thing upon himself.

An icicle smashed against the window she was looking out of. She hustled toward the door, slipping and skidding across a puddle left by the melting ice, almost falling down. She snatched back the bolt and flung open the inner door, leaving only the screen door between her and the hoods.

"You little bastards get outta here or I'll call the police!"

A snowball spattered against the screen door, spraying her with snow.

"You little bastards!" she screamed.

The whole neighborhood must have heard her, and before Jack could believe his eyes, she was out the door and after them. His barefoot, toothless, half-naked caterwauling mother charged down the back porch steps and through the snow in hot pursuit. And the hoods threw no more. They dropped everything, turned tail and ran, not looking back even once, putting all the territory they could between themselves and that screaming mimi, her cries terrorizing their hearts and minds as no police siren had ever done.

On the back porch the shivering, weeping, bleeding boy writhed in shame, waiting for her to stomp back inside, dreading to behold the twisted face of his deliveress. He wished himself dead, wished he could do himself in right there, but he knew from his catechism class that suicide was the most grievous sin of all in the eyes of the Lord.

DEWDROPS

1

TWO MEN ARE standing in front of an audience of around fifty people. The audience members—in many shapes, sizes, ages, genders, and gender preferences—sit in plastic chairs, most slouching, a sprinkling with perfect posture, some bent over with their elbows on their knees, a few thumbing through their notebooks, a few others whispering, one or two acting up and laughing, several with locked-in gazes of concentration or distress. They are arrayed in all manner of clothing, several even in bathrobes. But no hats and no sunglasses. Those are forbidden here.

One of the men, Peter, is short, his hair whitish-gray, wispy, disappearing. Although pudgy now, he carries the remains of a weightlifter's body—a square in transformation to round, like a boulder going soft at the edges. He wears a cotton crew-neck sweater with sleeves pushed up to his elbows, wrinkled khaki pants, loafers with no socks.

The other man, Ray, is tall, lanky, thin, almost too thin. He looks hungry. He wears jeans faded by many washings, a white Western shirt with silver snaps down the front, tan suede cowboy boots with multi-colored leather on the sides and tops, both the suede and the leather roughed up by long usage. His hair is dark and on the short side; one might call him well-groomed. He has the stance and the manner of a lone wolf watching the pack in the distance, his gaze a mixture of contempt and longing. His dark eyes say, "I see you, I see all of you."

Peter and Ray are examining something in Peter's hand, something metal, whispering to each other as they do. Peter looks up and takes a step forward. "My name is Peter. I'm an addict. My drug of choice was alcohol. That's what matters about me, nothing else. But for the newbies that maybe don't know me, I'm the executive director here. I noted at least ten of you were late, and the rest of you didn't say a damn thing to the late ones. It doesn't surprise me. Nobody cares, right?

"See this?" he nearly shouts as he raises the item in his hand for all to see. Many squint, trying to make it out. "Ted found it this morning while he was cutting the grass. It's a shaft, a hollow metal tube with a connecting bolt at the end. It's from one of the gas lines that run to the fireplaces in your cottages. The shaft, or whatever it is, I'm no mechanic, is hollow. The bolt is shaped like the bowl of a pipe. And that's exactly what one, or some of you, have done with it. Used it for a hash pipe!"

A couple of snorts, a guffaw, assorted chuckles.

"You think it's funny? What is wrong with you anyway?"

He brings the implement to his nose, sniffing. "The stuff in here is fresh. That means someone in this community has brought a drug onto these grounds and is using it here. It also means that one or more of you is keeping a secret. You know that someone is using, and you're not doing anything about it. That's how little you care. About this community. About yourselves. Secrets kill! When are you gonna figure that out? Yeah, I know you think it's harmless. Just a little grass. Just a little toke, a little sip, a couple pills, just one glass of wine with dinner, a snort, a poke. Same dumb-ass thinking that got you here. *Every* mood-altering chemical is poison in here.

He holds up the makeshift pipe again. "We're checking the cottages. Whichever one is missing this little item, we'll be talking to those people. And they'll likely be gone by tomorrow. I'm angry. Angry as hell. But mostly I'm scared. Do you know what this means? Someone has brought death into this place. This refuge. And *nobody cares!* This community is sick. The disease is winning here."

He stalks out of the room, leaving Ray alone in front of the assembled patients. There is more than the usual rustling and murmuring of a group in transition as they absorb the dread that Peter has left behind him hovering over the room. Ray stands still and quiet, his silence and patient stance becoming a command, and, indeed, after a few restless moments, the audience grows quiet with him—alert, apprehensive, unconsciously hoping that Peter's discordant exit note will be resolved in some reasonable way.

Ray turns to a whiteboard behind him and wheels it next to him. On it he writes:

Primary

Progressive

Chronic

"So," Ray says in a low, gentle voice, barely audible at the outset, and some of the audience must physically strain forward to hear him. "Here you are. Lost in the stars. One fine morning you set out on your voyage, and you took a wrong turn. You didn't know. You made a choice. But you didn't really know what the consequences would be. And you traveled through worlds of pain. And, finally, you were more asleep than awake, more dead than alive. But then you came to. By some miracle you woke up. Or someone woke you up. And suddenly you knew. And that was another miracle. That you knew. That you knew you were lost.

I know what you're thinking, I really do. You think you're alone. In your special, private world of pain. Your terminal uniqueness. But you're not alone anymore. I'm here now. And I know. Believe me, I know. My name is Ray. I'm an addict. My drugs of choice were alcohol and cocaine. This is the regularly scheduled lecture on the disease concept of addiction. It's probably the most important lecture you'll hear. I hope you listen. And please, for once in your lives, try to see what fits and not what doesn't.

When I tell you about this disease, I'm going to be telling your story. And my story too. I need to tell you my story, to open myself up to you, tell you who I am. We addicts are like oysters. We live alone in our shells. Just us and our drugs and our secrets. And we keep grinding away in there, trying to make a pearl. But no one can see the pearl unless we open up and let them see the oyster too, that slimy thing we are afraid we really are.

We live alone in the darkness, and we think we know. But we don't. We're dying in there. In our shells. In the darkness. We have to open up. Or we die. And so we need to tell our stories. I especially need to tell mine right now. Because I haven't been feeling so good lately. Oh yes, don't be surprised, it happens to us standing up here just like it does to you sitting out there. I haven't been feeling very well at all. I've been feeling trapped lately. And that's no good for me. Because then I get like old Huck Finn. I want to get on my raft and float on away. Light out for the territories. Escape. But there's no escape. Not for long anyway.

You do have a *dis*-ease. A *dis*-ease of the body, mind, and spirit. How does this disease work? Very simply. Once we take one drink, one snort, one smoke, one pill, one needle, we lose the power of choice entirely. We take ourselves hostage. We surrender ourselves to a process of enslavement and death. Eventually we become living corpses, estranged from all that gives life. All because we made that one terrible little choice.

How do you know if you have this disease? Again, it's simple. If continuing drug use causes problems in your life, you're an addict. It doesn't make any difference how often you use or how much you use. If you drink only one day a year, but that's the day you choose to rob the local convenience store, or beat your wife or your kids, or do anything negative or destructive that you wouldn't do if you were sober, you're an addict. Because you know what has happened before. And you know, despite lying to yourself to the contrary, that it's likely to happen again. But you still don't stop.

But we really don't just use one day a year, do we? We crave more and more. We always want more and more. We are insatiable. And we take more and more until we exhaust our own substance. That's what addiction is. It's a horror story, worse than any you've seen in the movies. It's like demon possession. Or vampires. Count Dracula. That's how I saw myself in the end. A creature of the night. Stalking, but not sure for what. Drugs, women, the 'Solution,' the 'Thing,' whatever it might be, that may just fill up the Black Hole of my Self, the Black Hole that sucked in everything—but with no real effect, never full, never enough.

The best description of how the disease of addiction works isn't in the medical journals. Go to a little book by Robert Louis Stevenson called *The Strange Case of Dr. Jekyll and Mr. Hyde.* Maybe you saw the old movie. Scary. Spencer Tracy. Gentle man. Fine man. Dr. Jekyll drinks a chemical and changes into Hyde—a monster, a human devil. Then, after a while, he turns into a monster even without taking the chemical. He's more monster than man now and has to take the chemical to *change back* into a human being. The chemical that made him a monster is now the only thing that can make him human again. Sound familiar? What does that do to your world view?

Primary. This disease is primary. Which means it is not caused by anything else. It's not caused by lack of willpower, at least after that first drink or snort or needle. It's not caused by psychological problems. You think you're crazy. You think you're evil. But most of us are just sick. We do some crazy—even evil—things. But only when we take the chemical. You take the chemical, and you become Mr. Hyde. In the first fifteen years of my life, before I took my first drug, I had no really big problems—jail-type problems. And in these last five years that I've been clean and sober, I haven't had those problems. But in the fifteen or so years in between I sure did. In the last five years I haven't stolen anything, corrupted anybody, or woken up from a blackout with no clue what I may have done the night before—who I might have slept with, hurt, maimed, killed. But when I was using, I was a very bad actor a lot of the time. I'm a convicted felon. A smuggler. A pusher. 'God Damn the Pusher Man.' Yes, eventually, just like Dr. Jekyll, you turn into Mr. Hyde even when you don't swallow what's in that beaker, even when you don't take the chemical.

What confuses us a lot is that we don't think this disease has anything to do with our bodies, that it's not biological like other diseases. But researchers have found that alcoholics secrete a different chemical in their brains when they drink alcohol than normal people do. So we're finding out that what we thought was a moral defect, or, at best, a form of mental defect has a physical, biological basis.

My parents were alcoholics. The old man took off when I was four years old, and I haven't seen him since, but I found out enough about him to know what he was. And my mother too. I spent my childhood moving around from one dingy little house to another with my mom and a succession of boyfriends and husbands, every one of them a drunk. But the important thing is not that I grew up with all those drunks. The important thing is that my parents *were* drunks. This disease runs in families. Families! I always thought families were nothing. Like gum on your shoes. All you had to do was scrape it off and go on. Just walk away.

But it isn't so simple. Everything we're finding out is telling us that addiction is usually inherited in some way. It turns out that some of us in this world *inherit a predisposition to addiction.* If I've got this defect in my genes, it doesn't mean I will become an addict for certain, or that I have to stay addicted. It just means that I have a greater chance of becoming an addict. Just bad odds. Yes, *inherited.* In the genes. Like a curse. Like original sin. Yes, some of us are born with a curse hanging over us. And, out there, thousands of addicts are dying of it every day. What does *that* do to your world view? . . .

2

RAY SITS AT his desk in his office. The desk is covered with neatly stacked piles of papers lined up in rows and columns. In front of his desk five plastic chairs are arranged in a semicircle. A couple of similar plastic chairs sit against one of the walls, along with a device called a "batacca," but which goes by several other names as well—an "encounter bat," for example. It has been used in some treatment centers in anger work. It looks like a tennis racket with a large, cushioned head, which is held high and brought down hard and flat against a specially made cushion with vinyl stretched tightly over it so that the batacca makes a loud *whack!* when it strikes the cushion.

To Ray's right is a large picture window. The other walls are covered with bookshelves stuffed with books of diverse sizes and subjects, and with paintings and drawings, most of which are gifts sent to him over the years from his former patients, some full of color, vivid and bright, some more subdued, others more like reified cries of anguish. On the wall behind him, hovering over him, hangs a large print of Winslow Homer's *Gulfstream*—a shirtless, barefoot black man lying on his back, trying to keep his small sailboat, its spar snapped off, from capsizing in the churning Caribbean sea. Shark fins splice the waters surrounding him. A typhoon looms on the horizon. In the distance a large ship is in sight, but too far away to come to his aid in time, even if it wanted to bother with the fate of one such as him.

The desk is L-shaped. A computer monitor sits on the long part of the "L" to Ray's right. He is working on one of the piles of papers. The phone rings. He picks up the receiver.

"Yes?"

He listens.

"You think it was him? I wouldn't be surprised. Well, we'll see."

He hangs up the phone and returns to his paperwork. The first of the scheduled encounter group arrives. Angel Day is her name, not her real name, but the only one that has mattered in a very long time. She has long, impossibly lush hair. Each feature of her face, her body, stands out, a singularity, but there is not a sharp angle anywhere. Everywhere holds a promise of softness, more a verdant landscape than a human thing, a mysterious place more than a person, a garden of earthly delights, a garden some would be pleased to die in. The rules here require her to suppress her sexuality, and she has even gestured toward a grudging compliance, but to little effect, because she has studied and displayed it for so long that it has captured every pore and cell of her and will not let go. She sits down in one of the chairs next to the open space in the center of the semicircle where Ray usually pulls up his chair. She stares at him, her eyes a periwinkle blue, beckoning him. He does not look up.

Finally, she says, "And good morning to you too."

He says, not looking up, "Things going okay for you?"

"Better. How could they be anything but better? I'm alive again. I even started to write a little song last night. I thought the music had gone away forever. Boy, that piano in the game room needs tuning bad."

"Did you play for anyone?" Ray asks.

"There were a few people around."

"Well, I have to tell you that scares me for you. Nix on that entertainment stuff. It's not real. Writing a song, that's okay. That's great. But that rock goddess stuff won't work for you now. Let it go. Turn your back on the worshipers. They're out to get you."

Her shoulders droop, and she says, a little mournfully, "It's hard. It's a habit. Second nature. They want, and I want them to want."

"That's wisdom. Hold onto it."

"Tell me something. When does it go away? The wantin'? Wantin' the drug? Sometimes…shit, right here today, you know, I got the blues. The nothin's. Those fuckin' nothin's just grabbed hold of me, and I wanted it. It drives me crazy. I don't want to want it. I really don't. But I do anyway. Christ!"

Ray nods. "It may never go away all the way. It still gets hold of me sometimes. More than I want to admit to myself. I just get that urge to light out for the territories, or go back to the caves, to that darkness I loved so much. Until it almost killed me."

"Jesus! After five years you still get the urge? I won't be able to take it."

"'One day at a time' for the rest of our lives. 'A daily reprieve based on our spiritual condition.' An AA cliché maybe, but that doesn't mean it isn't 100 percent true. That's all we'll ever have."

"What a drag," she says as she lifts her gaze toward the ceiling. Ray hears and notices. He frowns. He knows it is going to be hard to help her.

Duke saunters in—a studied saunter, a little too desperately telling the world he doesn't really buy into the nonsense of this whole place. He is a grizzled old veteran who affects a manner not unlike his namesake, dear old John Wayne himself, but unlike the cowboy hero, this Duke is more shrill than self-assured, more afraid than brave.

"Duker!" says Angel, who has genuine affection for him, as she does for almost everyone.

"Angel baby!"

"You ready to do some work today, Duker?" Pointing to the batacca, she says, "I wanna see ya beat on that cushion, boy."

"Shit. I may be crazy, but I ain't nuts."

Paula and Maggie enter together and sit next to each other. Paula wears glasses and is on the cusp between pudgy and fat. She is eager, caring, sorrowful but hopeful, manifesting an innocence too foolish.

Like Ray, Maggie is all sharp angles, lean and wolfish. Her dress, hairstyle, her entire look— is androgynous, not because she is that way but because she chooses to see herself and be seen that way. Her neuterness is her gauntlet thrown down.

Angel, snubbing Maggie, says "Hi, Paula."

"Hi, Angel."

Ray looks up from his paperwork and at his watch. "Time to start. We're running real late."

He slides his chair from behind the desk into the circle, avoiding the empty space next to Angel, making a place between Maggie and Paula instead. Maggie reluctantly moves her chair to accommodate him.

He asks, "Has anyone seen Billy?"

"I just had a smoke with him," says Duke.

"We'll have to start without him."

The group members rise from their chairs and begin hugging each other. Angel hugs Ray first, leaning into him, but he bends himself backward and moves his legs to avoid her. He breaks off the hug. Duke can't stand this hugging business, which he performs so perfunctorily that it amounts to a refusal. Maggie and Paula hug long and lovingly, which Duke observes with a disgust obvious to all. Billy enters the room and tries to melt inconspicuously into the scene. They finish the hugs and return to their chairs.

Ray looks around, a quick visual survey of the group.

"Who's ready to work?" he says.

An awkward silence prevails until Angel can't stand it any longer. "We're getting a new one today, huh?"

"Another big shot," says Duke. "Got himself a fancy robe and pajamas."

"Boy, is he shell-shocked," says Billy. "Chugalugged a pint of Jack Daniels on the way from the airport ta come down off the coke. Hit the sack like a rock. Puked in the bed."

Duke snorts a laugh. "One sick puppy dog today."

Ray interrupts. "Let's cut the bull, gang. Who's ready to work?"

Silence. Again. Uncomfortable.

"So you want me to drag it out of you again. This group is in bad shape. It scares me."

He turns and faces Billy. "Why were you late?"

"I guess I just didn't follow the time."

"Bull. You're late most of the time. It's deliberate. Your way of showing us something. What? Anger? Contempt? Your way of getting right at the center of our universe. Do you want to work on that?"

The ensuing silence is weighted with a sullen heaviness. There is a squirm or two. None of them want to enjoy what is happening to Billy; they can take no joy in his discomfort; they might just be next.

Alex wanders in wearing a robe and pajamas splattered with vomit stains. He wears loafers with no socks. His hair sticks up in places where he has slept on it. He carries a folder.

"Hello," Ray says.

"I don't know if I'm in the right place."

Angel says with a friendly little cackle of a laugh, "You're in exactly the right place, darlin'."

"Pull up a chair, Alex," Ray says. "And"—indicating the folder in Alex's hand—"I'll take that."

Alex, self-conscious and hesitant, drags a chair into the circle and sits down.

"What are you feeling right now?" Ray asks.

"Feeling?"

"Yes, feeling."

"Conspicuous."

"You mean ashamed. That's a disguised way to say you're feeling shame."

Alex touches his hair. "They wouldn't let me have my hair dryer. Said they had to check it out. For what? For defects? For hidden drugs? I don't know." He looks down at his robe and pajamas. "And I've got to get this stuff washed. Why do I have to wear this stuff anyway? Everybody else has clothes on."

"Didn't they tell you why, Alex? That we want you to understand when you come in here that you're sick?"

"How dumb. Makes no sense."

"And everything's got to make sense to you, right?"

Alex shrugs, feeling his way carefully in this strange new world.

"You think you can just watch and listen for a while, let us come back to you later?"

"Sure."

Ray turns to Billy. "Billy, the hash pipe came from your cottage."

There are a few moments of silence, even more uncomfortable than before.

"So what?"

"Was it your hash pipe, Billy?"

"No. But what if it was? There ain't nothin' wrong with a little grass. You people are full of shit."

"Rigorous honesty, Billy. That's what it's all about. You made a pact, a covenant, when you came in here."

"Are you accusing me?"

Ray sits silent.

"You son of a bitch," Billy says.

"Come on, Billy, settle down," Duke says.

"Fuck you, Ray," Billy says. "Fuck this whole God-damn place."

He jumps up and heads for the door.

"Oh, no," Paula says, barely audible.

"Billy!" Angel starts after him.

"Stay here, Angel," Ray says sternly.

"I'm gonna talk to him. I can keep him here."

Maggie says, "Yeah, dangle that little honey pot in front of him."

"Fuck you, Maggie."

Pointing to her chair, Ray says to Angel, "Sit down. We've got work to do here. Life and death work. And we can't do it if we're chasing after Billy."

"He might not get back again."

"No, he might not. They're dying all over the world out there."

Angel reluctantly sits down. Ray moves to his desk, picks up the phone, hits a button.

"Peter, I've got a runner. Billy. I confronted him. He took off."

Ray listens for a moment. "That's what I thought. Try to hit him with that before he leaves, or he'll go out of here thinking he's gotten away with it. By the time he gets to town he'll be believing his own bullshit again."

Ray hangs up the phone and moves back into the circle. "It was Billy's hash pipe. His roommate told. You see, Angel, you can't keep him here because he hasn't really been here. Maybe he'll even stay, but I doubt it. He isn't ready for our help."

Alex is agitated. Ray turns to him. "What's going on with you? What are you feeling right now?"

"Feeling?"

"Feeling."

"Well, I think…"

"Stop. That's not a feeling. That's a judgment."

"I guess I'm confused. Frustrated."

"You mean angry. Forget the big words, the complicated words. You're either mad, glad, sad, guilty, ashamed, afraid, or hurt."

"You accused that kid. Then he runs out. You don't care if he leaves, goes back out and uses again. I think that's wrong. What are you here for anyway?"

"So you're mad."

"That's not the point."

"That's the whole point. Where's the anger coming from?"

"The injustice. It's not fair."

"Or does it come from your own hurt?"

"It's no skin off my back. It's just wrong, that's all. You're supposed to be helping people, but it seems like you're just fucking with them. Is that what this place is about?"

"So you're a defender of mankind. Is that what you are?"

Alex sulks. "Maybe."

"Someone wasn't fair to you, right?"

"Oh come off that shit. That's a crock."

"When a new member joins the group, we ask her or him to introduce himself or herself, tell us a little bit about themselves, about their family, about their drug use, how they got here, what their expectations are. Are you willing to do that? Are you willing to tell us who you are?"

"What about the kid?"

"Yes, if we talk about him, we won't have to talk about you, right?"

Shrugging, reluctantly playing along, Alex says, "Well, I'm a lawyer…"

"Okay, that's what you do. That's not who you are."

"Word games, huh? I can play those too."

"I'll bet you can. But please, instead, just tell us who you are."

Alex thinks for a moment, wondering where to begin. "I had a decent enough childhood. I was adopted…"

Again Ray interrupts, "You mean you were abandoned."

"No, adopted."

"If you were adopted, you had to be abandoned first."

Alex looks down, taking it in, then raises his head. "I guess I never thought of it that way. I don't even remember my real parents. I don't know if anybody even knew who my father was. My mother kept me until I was almost two, then gave me up. But somebody took me in. I was lucky there, I guess. At least that's what they told me all the time. Good people. Religious people. Stern people. Dull, mean people. They broke lots of yardsticks over my ass. They counted them. What did people like that want a kid for in the first place?"

"But just a minute ago you said you were lucky."

"Better than what happened to a lot of foster kids…When I got out of grade school, they sent me away to boarding school. And at the boarding school I discovered some more about the way the world really is. Those kids were cruel, and I was one of them, one of the leaders. We would band to-gether and exclude, cast out the odd ones, the stupid ones, the ugly ones. But I got sick of it, sick of myself for being part of it. So I just walked away. Not completely. I still stayed in their world. *In* it, though I tried not to be *of* it, if you know what I mean. I wasn't going to risk failure. Even when I was a little kid walking down the street, walking past people, they wouldn't notice me at all, but I'd be saying to myself, but really talking to them, 'You just wait. You're gonna hear from me someday.'" He cocks his back and head in a gesture of recognition and regret. "I always wanted to do something for the world…"

"*For* the world or *in* the world, Alex? Something the world would take notice of…remember you for?"

"I guess so. I guess that was it all the time. And I tried, you know, to find the answer in books, all the modern despair stuff, all the anti-heroes, all the hatred of life. And I guess that brought out what was inside me all the time…that I hated life too…"

"Do you believe in God, Alex?"

"If God exists, He's evil."

Paula gasps.

Ray flashes a flicker of annoyance at Paula but quickly shrugs it off. "Why do you say that? Because it doesn't make sense to you?"

"Yes, that. And the babies in the frying pans…" Alex pauses, waiting for a question. But Ray says nothing. "You know, the parents who fry up their babies like bacon…"

"Oh my God!" Paula bursts out.

"Yeah, they really do it. I was involved in a case like that once." He visibly shudders. "Horrible."

"Sons of bitches," says Duke.

"Anyway, I worked my way through college. Still graduated early. Always a big success. Because I was afraid to fail. But I was miserable still. Depressed all the time. It seemed like I was an alcoholic even then. It just took some time for it to work itself out. It's hard for me to say this, but I wanted to be a poet once. But every time I'd sit down to write, nothing would come. Except autobiographical shit. Maudlin trash. Who cares about that shit anyway? And then when I'd try to look outside of myself, what was there to say about *that*? That out there, that infernal machine out there, chewing, grinding, regurgitating…garbage, trash, shit, nothing but shit, and turning the people into shit too. Overwhelmed, powerless, ground to dust. I couldn't speak. If I ever had a voice, I lost it.

"So I became a lawyer. The idea was to help people. I was a civil rights lawyer. School desegregation was my main cause. But it was like Sisyphus…just pushing a big rock up a hill and watching it roll back down again. Eventually I went for the money. My clients loved me. I became a real estate wizard. I showed them how to swallow up the earth. And I hated it. But I still did it. I still hate it. I'm still doing it. Shucking, jiving, prevaricating, manipulating, dominating. And all for what? Mercedes, Porsches, BMWs? Two-thousand dollar suits? Swallowing up the God-damn world for a Mercedes Benz and a two-thousand-dollar suit."

"Do you have a family?"

"Oh. Oh, I forgot them, didn't I? Just gum on my shoes, that's all they were to me. We're separated. Two kids. I just walked away." He buries his face in his hands.

Ray says, "Abandoned them."

And after he lets that sink in, "And the booze? The drugs?"

"Mostly booze. I was a drunk from the first drink...

Several of the group members mumble "yeah" or "same here," nodding their heads in the affirmative.

"But I never seemed to lose anything. Anything external. Anything material. But my soul, my heart, or whatever it is in here, was shriveling up. And then one night a couple of years ago, driving drunk, I hit someone walking in the street. At least I think I did. I took off. Hit and run. I was drunk enough that night I convinced myself it didn't happen and went to sleep. But next morning I saw there was a dent on my car that nothing but a body could have made and what looked like drops of blood. They never caught me. No one ever knew, until now, until this moment. And I still don't know what happened. Christ! It was the loneliest street in the world. I was drunk. I wasn't paying attention. Where did that person come from? Why was he walking in the damn street? I still don't know what really happened. Is the person dead? Maimed? Maybe I'm a murderer. I wanted all my life to help people, but that's sure not the way it turned out."

"And how did you get here?"

"Well, last year I discovered cocaine."

"Uh-oh," says Angel.

"Sounds like you know the rest of the story. At first it was just a cure for my hangovers. I was on a binge last week. Camped out in a hotel. Drinking, snorting, drinking, snorting. Cocaine and Jack Daniels. That's all I was doing at the end. And whores sometimes, two at a time. A couple of my law partners, my wife, even though we're separatd, and an old friend of mine who's an AA member, they came to the hotel. They said they loved me. And I was standing there at the window, looking out into the night, like I'd done every other night for such a long damn time, wondering when it was all going to be over for me. And then my friend said, 'Why won't you surrender, Alex? Please, please, for God's sake surrender.' And I guess I did surrender. Some anyway. I thought, why are these people doing this? They say they love me. I am the slime of the earth, and they say they love me. How could they possibly love me?"

Ray says, "And now that you're here, what do you expect to happen?"

"I don't know. I guess I just want to find a way...to live, to find some meaning, to be real. Coming out here on the plane, drunk and delirious as I was, I thought, okay, Alex, maybe you can find God or something like God out there in the West...in the mountains out there," nodding his head toward the window.

"The God you say is evil? Is that who you're looking for?"

"I'll take what I can get."

"Okay, Alex. What you've been doing we call 'work' here. You've been working. Working hard. After someone works, after someone opens up his mind and heart and soul for us to see, then we ask him if he is willing for the other members of the group to say what they have seen. You've told your tale, or tried to, the best way you know how, for now. And they have heard you. What did they hear? What did they see? Are you willing to hear from the group, Alex?"

"I guess so."

"Who has a gift for Alex? That's what they are, Alex, even if they don't seem like gifts at first. If you don't much care for them at first, like the unfashionable tie or ill-fitting sweater your aunt gives you for Christmas, just put them in the back of the closet. They might come into fashion or fit better someday, or you might just change your mind about them."

Again there is a long silence, and, again, Angel must break it.

"I don't know. Listening to you, it's like you've got it all figured out, but then it doesn't do you any good. I'm glad you're here. You need to be here. You belong here."

"And how about you?" Ray says. "Tell Alex about yourself."

"My name is Angel. Angel Day."

"The singer?" Alex says. "God, I wondered when I saw you..."

"The one and only."

"Yeah, Alex," Duke says, "we got 'em all here. Singers, big shots, queers like Maggie over there. We got every kind of jackoff, bonehead, goofball, and rockhead that ever walked on this earth."

Maggie erupts. "Ray, how long are you gonna let him get away with this?"

"I can't protect you from him forever, Maggie."

"Thanks for nothing."

"Duke," Ray says sharply, "you're totally out of bounds. You know the rules…"

"Yeah, I do; I take it back; sorry, Maggie," he says with no sincerity. "Can I finish now?" He waits for Ray to stop him, but Ray does not. "Yeah, Alex, I ain't nothin' special like the rest of these fine specimens here. I'm just a garden variety drunk named Duke. I've worked like a dog all my life in the oil fields. I'm here 'cause I got drunk one night and beat on the lady of the house a little bit. She just didn't know when to shut the fuck up."

He chuckles at his joke. Nobody else does.

"My lawyer thought that goin' to this funny farm would be a good idea. So I could tell the judge it was just the booze, and now I've straightened myself out and all that happy horseshit. Ought to be good for a suspended sentence. So I'm just doin' my time."

Ray says, "So now he knows who you are. Who is he?"

"Well, to be completely honest, I can't rightly say that I understood a word he said. Basically he's full of shit. Like all the rest of us. But I like him anyhow."

"I like *you*," Ray corrects Duke. "You're talking to Alex."

"Shit, he knows what I mean. And I'll bet he's a damn good lawyer when he isn't pissin' and moanin' and cryin' in his beer. All that about swallowin' up the earth. Shit, Alex, you'll be just fine when you accept the simple fact that the earth was made to fuck, just like I do every day with that oil rig I work on. Pump the old stuff out of her 'til there ain't no more left. That's what we were made for, counselor. So welcome to the bug house. And don't let the bastards get you down."

It is quiet again. For too long. The group looks furtively at each other. Finally, Paula ventures, warily, almost inaudibly, "You made me cry, Alex. But I always cry when I hear the stories."

"Alex, this is Paula," says Ray. "And Paula is a victim, a victim who won't confront what's happened to her. Paula, you've been here five weeks now, and you still haven't worked on your father."

Paula shakes her head no.

"If you don't deal with him before you leave, I don't give you a snowball's chance of staying straight."

"That's true," says Maggie. She puts her hand on Paula's knee as Duke snorts in disgust. "You have to exorcize that demon, honey."

"I know."

"You don't want to let go of him, do you, Paula?" Ray asks.

"I must be crazy."

"That's what *he* wants you to believe," says Ray. "Are you ready now? We have time now. We're ready to help you, Paula."

She shakes her head violently no.

"You've got to do it, Paula. Very soon. It's getting time for you to go home."

"I don't want to go."

"But you have to go. Reality, Paula. That's what we have to face. We can't stay in our shells."

Paula keeps shaking her head no, no, no.

Ray, giving up for now, turns to Maggie. "What about you?"

"Okay," she says reluctantly, "but you don't really want to hear this." She lifts her chest and neck and chin, sitting straight and poised, narrows her eyes to slits, and turns to Alex. "Self-pity. That's what I heard. I know your type. I was married to a type like you once. I don't know what to tell you. The truth is those aren't problems you've got.

That's just a bunch of intellectual shit in your head. You've just read too many books. But your wife, she's the one with problems. Raised to be a concubine. I know because I was that too. Stuck with two kids. What's she have now? Maybe some parents that think she ought to run out and marry another one like you. I can tell you, the girls in the Junior League don't want her around anymore. Maybe she can be a sales clerk in a boutique, or a secretary."

"Oh shit," says Angel. "She's on the soapbox again."

"Maggie," says Ray, "that's just destructive."

"I hope so."

"What about you? Who are you?"

"I'm a hag, a shrew, a banshee, a harpie, a castrater, a witch, a dyke. What I am is a second-class human being because I was born with a hole between my legs. And what I am is a perpetual pain in the ass to everyone around me because I don't like it, and I can't help telling people I don't like it. And, most of all, what I am is sick and tired and disgusted. And I want out of your world, Alex. I tried to get out of your world. See these?" She holds up her wrist to show the scars. "I tried to get out, Alex. But I'm not even that free. I don't even have that right. No! Pricks like him"—pointing to Ray—"decide to 'save' me. Drag me in here. Call me an addict. Bullshit! My problem is that I know, I see, and I hate. And I will not be reconciled. You hear that, Ray? I will not be reconciled. I will not be brainwashed or lobotomized. You won't send me out of here to be a good little girl, a so-called productive member of society. Go save the rest of the God-damn world and leave me alone."

"Go out there to die?" says Ray. "What do you prove by dying, Maggie?"

"That I refused."

"And on your tombstone the epitaph will be what? Victim? Martyr? Scapegoat? What a lousy thing to die for."

"Says you. And who the fuck are you anyway?"

"Just another pilgrim. Another pilgrim looking for a refuge. Is there no refuge for you, Maggie?"

"None. No refuge. And no refuge for you either, Ray. I heard your story. Unreconciled. A goner just like me. A fucked duck. Your words aren't working for you anymore, are they? What are you gonna do when the words don't work for you anymore?"

"I don't know, Maggie. I guess I'll have to keep working to keep that from happening."

He looks at his watch. "But we're almost done for this session, and it's Alex's moment now."

He turns to Alex. "I feel like I met my own brother here today. You told a lot of my story too. You said you were looking for some meaning here. For 'something like God,' you said. I don't know if you'll find God here, but I hope you stop looking. For God or any of the rest of it—the Answer, the green light. You know what the green light is? You need to remember, Alex. I'm sure you've read *Gatsby*. Remember the end? 'Gatsby believed in the green light, the orgiastic future that year by year recedes before us. It eluded us then, but that's no matter. Tomorrow we will run faster, stretch out our arms farther...So we beat on, boats against the current...' Fitzgerald was an alcoholic. He knew. Get in touch with your pain. Get in touch with what it's meant for you to be abandoned, a stranger, a refugee. Get in touch with what it's meant to have abandoned others, to have hurt others. The old cycle repeating itself again and again. The victim becomes the oppressor. You have some unfinished business with a little boy. You'll never find him out there in the stars. You might think that's some magnificent, tragic search. But it's not. It's just an escape. An escape into yet another trap, another maze, another illusion."

He turns suddenly to Angel. "And I want you to think about why you needed to tell Alex your last name. We don't have last names here."

"I..."

"I didn't say I wanted you to talk about it. I said I wanted you to think about it."

"But…"

"Time's up. Let's close."

They all stand, Alex slowly following the others, unfamiliar with the procedure, slightly behind everyone else. They form a circle, arms around each other's shoulders, and say aloud, "God grant me the serenity to accept the things I cannot change, courage to change the things I can, and wisdom to know the difference."

They leave, except for Angel, who says, "That was a lousy thing to do."

"That's one way not to think about it," Ray says.

"Okay. You're right again."

"I don't want to be right. I just want you to get well."

"Why?"

Ray, confused, "Why?"

"Another notch on your gun belt? Another reason you can give yourself to keep on going? But then, what if I don't want to get well? What do we do then, Ray?"

"I don't believe it. You're here, aren't you?"

"We might just both be doomed, Ray. It's just that I know it and you don't."

"I hope not, Angel. I hope not."

"You know, I think I love you."

"And I love you too."

"Like you love all these drunks and junkies. I'm not talkin' about that. I mean love. I mean I want you. I want to be with you. Now. And beyond."

"The shrinks call that transference. It happens all the time. You fall in love with your therapist. It passes."

"And that's bullshit. I've been to ten shrinks and didn't give a rat's ass about any of them. And I've known all the kinds of men in the world. Most of them were nothin'…or mostly nothin'. But you're somethin'.

Will you tell me the truth? Like you say, 'rigorous honesty'? Do you ever sit over there and just want to hold me? Does that ever cross your counselor mind? Not fuck me. Just hold me?"

He laughs. "That, ma'am, is a consummation maybe devoutly to be wished but never to be had."

"Well, what that is, is a yes, and that's everything."

"It's not a yes. Because there's a little thing called counselors' ethics. No fucking the patients."

"We can wait 'til I get out."

"Not for at least a year after, that's the rule."

"Screw that."

"Can't wait? We addicts can never wait, can we?"

"Why should we? What do they pay you? It must be dog shit. Hell, I'll buy you your own rehab center if you want. Give it to you, free and clear."

"You're missing the point. The reason for that rule is you're sick. You have a disease that wants to kill you. And you have to heal. And you can't heal if you're all tangled up with the damn guy who's supposed to be standing outside you and helping you see who you are."

"Save your breath. I already know who I am. And you know too. And you want me. I've known it from the first week."

"And so I might, Angel. So I might. And that makes me nothing special. Because everybody does. Who could help it? Not me anyway. Look at you. Listen to your music. You're all my unfinished business. And that's very bad shit, because now we've got a secret. You know what I have to do now? I have to go to Peter and tell him about this. You'll have to transfer to another group."

"I won't. I'll leave first."

"So be it."

"Okay. If you want to be a dumb fuck, go right ahead. But you're kidding yourself. I've heard your story, and like it or not, you've met your fate, and she's standing right here in front of you. All your life—before the drugs, with the drugs, after the drugs, all those things you talk about right here in this room every day—looking for the rainbow, the pot of gold, the green light. You can bullshit the others maybe, but you can't bullshit the bullshitter. I'm the rainbow, darlin'. I'm the pot of gold. I'm the green light."

She moves toward him. "Will you hold me?" She tries to put her arms around him. He freezes, crosses his arms protectively, but does not push her away. She hears someone coming and breaks away.

"Trust me. If you tell Peter, I'm gone"—she snaps her fingers—"like that."

3

"HI, ANGEL," PETER says as she passes him in the doorway on her way out. He backs up to let her through, watches her walk away down the hall, then closes the door to Ray's office. "Angry lady. God forgive me, Ray, for even thinking it, but have you ever seen anything finer in your life?"

"Probably not."

"But a poisoned cup if there ever was one. That was the toughest thing about being a counselor for me. All those pathetic little wounded girls. You know"—mimicking a Southern belle—"'Peter, if you could just fuck me, everything would be all right.' What bullshit. Thank God I passed. Why do we want to drink from those poisoned cups?"

"Maybe we're the poison in the cups."

"Well, maybe. But I think you *do* know. I wasn't here when she came in. I would never have assigned her to you. She belongs in Darla's group. I chewed their asses in Admissions when I found out. But it was too late to change. What was I going to say? 'Angel, I'm afraid you'll seduce my best counselor?' And give you a vote of no-confidence? But that's exactly what I should have said. How are you handling it?"

"So far, so good."

"You don't sound so sure. Like the window washer who fell off his pulley at the thirty-first floor. On his way down, about the twentieth floor, he says, 'So far, so good.'"

Ray laughs. "Maybe it was meant to be. Something she and I both need to deal with."

"Fuck that. No need to tempt fate. No need to taunt the gods. We're always wanting to do that. Are you hearing me?"

"Loud and clear."

"The phones have been ringing off the hook since she came in. National publicity. She'll put us over the top. A full house all the time. Everything we've wanted. And I don't want it to end with the wrong headline. 'Angel Day Shacks Up with Her Drug Counselor.' Then we're down the tube. Right down the tube."

Ray shudders. "Got it. No way."

"But that's not even the point, Ray. I don't want you to die. I love you. You're the best I've ever seen. You have the gift, but that means you're always walking right on the edge of the cliff. Very scary."

Ray does not respond. He does not know what to say.

"This place is a God-damn zoo lately. Sick. Worse than I've ever seen it. Everybody who isn't using or fucking is wanting to use or fuck. When we can't feel any other way, we try to feel with something else, eh?"

Ray has drifted away. "Hey, you've gone quiet," Peter says. "You okay?"

"I think so."

"Anything you want to tell me? Anything you want to talk about?"

"I don't think so."

"I don't know if I believe you. We're only as sick as the secrets we keep. I don't have to tell *you* that, do I?"

Ray shakes his head slowly, too slowly. "No."

"You sold that God-damn boat yet?"

"Not yet. Can't get my price."

"Fuck your price! That's old business. Drug money bought that boat. It's evil."

"Give me a break. That boat's got my life savings in it."

61

"I can't believe you're saying that. Those life savings of yours were purchased with the currency of death, buddy, and that boat'll be the death of you if you don't get rid of it."

"I haven't been on that boat in five years."

"Shit, Ray, since when are you so dumb to bullshit yourself like that? There's something in that past life of yours you don't want to let go of, something you want to fall back on when reality's just too hard to face. It's that illusion of escape you won't let go of, that Huck Finn shit you talk about, that lighting out for the territory shit. Here's a gift for you, like it or not. Cut the fucking price and sell the fucking boat. Better yet, give it away. Or scuttle it. Sink it to the bottom of the God-damn sea."

Peter pauses, trying to assess the effect of his words on the passive face before him.

"And it's time you gave up this job. I'm still saving that marketing job, but I can't save it forever. More money. Out of the line of fire. You should take it today. You're a born salesman. I'll take over this group until we can hire a new counselor."

"Born salesman! That's like a knife in my heart. I need to be right here in this room where the action is."

"Action. Shit on action. Day after day you're wallowing in their pain. What's that doing for you?"

Ray is bristling now, his voice threatening. "Maybe, Peter, I'm looking for some evidence— some evidence that this thing we call life and death isn't just some big cosmic ratfuck—evidence that it's something more than Darwin told us it was—'the dreadful but quiet war of creatures in the peaceful woods and smiling fields.'"

"You really memorize all that shit, don't you? Well, fuck that too. You keep wanting it to make sense, don't you? Well, hear the news, Ray. Maybe it's not ever going to make any sense. They gave you a birth certificate and a birthday suit and that's all, buddy. Be grateful for what you've got, help who you can, and fuck the rest of it."

"That thinking worked for me for a while, but it's not working for me anymore."

"So you've gone back into your shell. Introspecting. Grinding away in the darkness, trying to make that pearl again. That's death for us."

"I know. Maybe once I'm past this group I've got now, I'll do better. It seems tougher than any group I've ever had. Almost every one of them is a victim. Abused and abandoned children who've fashioned their victimhood into a suit of armor. And they think that armor is protecting them from even worse things than they've already suffered. And maybe it is. But at the same time it's suffocating them."

"Some wounds can never be healed, just bandaged up."

"I can't accept that."

"You mean you *won't* accept it."

"That's right. I won't. And maybe I've reached the end of *my* rope. Sometimes I just stand here at the window and look out there. And I want. I just want. Maybe I'm using them to keep me alive. I live with despair every day, but then some little thing happens in here that makes me want to keep on going just for a little while longer."

"They say if we don't grow we die. Are you growing, Ray?"

"No. But I don't know what else to do but keep on slogging, try to struggle on through."

"Maybe I'll have to make you take that marketing job. Kick you upstairs. Up or out. Would you let me do that?"

"Am I an addict?"

"Out?"

"Out."

"So you're in a trap, and you want me to come in there with you. Well, I decline the invitation. I'm going to think about it a little while longer, but I think that's exactly the choice I'm going to give you. And not much longer. A few days. A week at the most. Up or out. You're burning out. You've crossed the line, and pretty soon we're not going to be able to tell the difference between you and the patients. Ray will just disappear. There'll be nothing left of him but the pain he feels for others."

Peter looks at his watch and abruptly stands up. "I want a hug." They hug. Peter starts to leave, then turns back.

"Can I give you another gift?"

"Sure."

"We're like moths. Moths to flame. I see you dancing around the flames. And we weren't made for flames, buddy. We were made to lie down in green pastures."

4

. . . "YES," RAY CONTINUES, gesturing at the whiteboard and repeating, "what's *that* do to your world view? Out there addicts by the thousands—who knows how many—are dying every day." Some in the audience writhe at this thought, shaking their heads and making scoffing sounds of protest, regret, disgust. He continues, stifling any rising protest. "Progressive. This disease is progressive. And fatal. It gets worse over time, and it ends in death. Early death. It kills in all sorts of ways. Cirrhosis, car accidents, murder, suicide. But it wasn't the thought that I was dying that was so awful for me. It was having to *live* death. Right out of the horror movies. We become vampires, the living dead.

It doesn't start out that way. It didn't start out that way for me. At first it seemed to give me life, to fill up that void, that Black Hole that had been in me since I was a little boy. It let me celebrate. 'Dance beneath the diamond sky with one hand waving free' and all that crap."

Laughter sifts through the audience. Ray smiles.

Life should be a celebration, right? A lifting up? Soaring? It let me talk. It let me laugh away the willies, laugh at that damn Boogie Man. It let me hurl my words at the savage gods. I couldn't seem to talk without the booze. The booze let me let go. My heart, my tongue, were blocks of ice, and the booze melted them and let the poems in me flow. At least that's what I thought. But that void space in me, that Black Hole, was really just getting bigger all the time.

I don't know exactly when it turned on me, like it does to every addict. I got married, had a child, a daughter, went through graduate school, got a university teaching job. Maybe the wife and kid, the sense of moving forward, of life still being incomplete, kept me straight for a long time. But my wife, she was just a sweet girl I'd somehow picked up along the way. I didn't deserve her, and she sure as hell didn't deserve me. She just wanted fairly simple things—kids, a family life. Dull. Not me. Not me. I was too wonderful for that. I needed excitement. More and more all the time. Because nothing was ever enough.

I just took off one night. Drunk, of course. Propelled my wonderful self into the universe. We confuse freedom with escape. Oh the next day! The hangover willies. Like a mad dog, shaking and whining. But I got drunk again real quick and called my department chair and my wife. 'I can't do it,' I said. 'I'm crazy. I'm evil. You're better off without me.' She wanted to work it out somehow. Not me. I had written my script. The tragedy, or the melodrama, or whatever it was, had to go on. So, like my old man before me, I abandoned my wife and child.

Somehow I got another teaching job. Some fool hired me. A girl's college. I thought I'd died and gone to heaven. Angels everywhere..."

Ray catches himself, realizing he has used the wrong word in this particular situation. He stammers and seems to have forgotten what he intended to say next. A few in the audience understand what has happened, including Angel, whose "Ha!" of a laugh sounds above the others.

"So...So...I brought my sickness in there and started infecting others. As it got worse, it got all tied up with sex. Another way to try to escape the despair. The obsession with sex. What's the connection? Not that we're the only ones. Look at the culture. It's fuck-crazy. Listen to how we talk. Fuck this. Fuck that. Fuck it. I wonder if it's because that's all we've got left to try and feel with. A remembrance of wonder. But it can't bear the weight. Nothing can bear that weight. So it becomes just another commodity, then garbage, trash, pornography. Just another way to jack off. We're always looking for that peak experience, the big thrill that might just make us want to keep on going. 'The orgiastic future' Fitzgerald called it in *Gatsby*. Insatiable. Searching for the answer. *The answer*. I gotta have *the answer*.

Well, I was out of control. No celebrations now. Drinking just to stay alive. But I still had hope. It's so hard to kill the hope. Fitzgerald again, our whole world summarized in a paragraph, 'So we beat on, boats against the current.' Chasing after something. That remembrance of wonder? And then I discovered—*it*! Magic dust. Cocaine. Just in time. It cured my alcoholism. All that guilt and shame? No more. Gone. Snort some coke, and you are in control. For half an hour, you are master of the universe. The gods walk the earth again. Resurrection!

But I couldn't afford it. So I started dealing. Then I started smuggling. The 'Pusher Man.' Big money. Who needed to do dull-ass honest work? Crime pays. You could make thousands, hundreds of thousands, millions if you didn't get caught or killed. I bought my own boat. A real yacht it was too. I lived on it. What a life! Huck Finn himself. What I'd wanted all my life. Escape. Turned my back on the world. Nobody had a hold on me anymore. And I don't like to talk much about that old life. Because even after all the years and all the pain, it *still* pulls me back. Me on that boat, that big old raft, just drifting on the sea of the world. And one by one, all over the world, the lights twinkle out, and Ray is alone.

You see, I'm still an addict." He gestures toward the whiteboard. "It's a *progressive* disease. If we go back, it's even worse. That's why we can't go back. Ever. No matter what. But sometimes I just want to ease the pain a little. Get lost for a day or two. Find a cheap and easy way to lift up my heart. But I can't. Reality, that's where I have to stay, no matter how tough it seems to get sometimes. I say '*seems* to get' because it really isn't out there. It's in our minds, the way we react to the world.

The booze, the cocaine, the smuggling, the danger. You can get addicted to danger too. That peak experience. I kept taking risks. That's all there was left to live for. Because, without the risk, life was just pure shit. An open sore. Rubbing. Rubbing all the time. I had made my escape, but even that didn't satisfy me. That void, that black hole still kept getting bigger and bigger all the time, swallowing up everything that came near it—that came near me. Everything. And everyone.

Maybe I was desperately searching for defeat. Maybe that's what we need to be human, to become human—defeat. Well, I found it. A couple of junkies sneaked onto my boat to steal my stash and carved me up like a Thanksgiving turkey. Check it out…"

He rips open his shirt. Rope-like, purple scars crisscross his chest and belly.

The audience erupts in gasps, expletives, cries of "Jesus Christ!" "My God!" "Ray"! "What the fuck!"

But Ray does not pause. "This disease is fatal. It was a miracle I lived. But those junkies were real malicious bastards, because they left just enough drugs on that boat so I got put away for a couple of years. Prison. And yes, it's as bad as you've heard. But as awful as that prison was, I became thankful for it. Because I'd escaped the horror that my life had become. Yes. Escaped to prison. Utter defeat . . .

5

IN RAY'S OFFICE the group, except for Alex, is assembled, waiting. Alex—cleaned up now, looking more like his lawyerly self now—arrives with Joey in tow. Joey wears dark shades, a ball cap turned backward, frayed robe and pajamas, tennis shoes that are torn and grubby. Like Alex when he first came to the group, Joey carries a folder.

"Group, this is Joey," Alex says.

Angel, in her usual way, says "Welcome, darlin'."

"Hi, Joey," says Paula eagerly.

Duke, disgusted, looks away. Maggie is impassive. Ray points to two chairs next to him. Joey and Alex sit down.

"Joey, huh?" says Ray.

Joey very slowly nods his head. "You betcha."

"Not Joe?" Ray asks. "Joey?"

"Joey it sure is, bro."

Ray, indicating the sunglasses, says, "You hiding behind those things?"

Joey, in a loud whisper, says, "Yeah, but don't tell nobody, bro. Nobody in here but us chickens, man."

"You're gonna have to take them off. We try not to hide from each other in here."

"Groovy." Joey takes off the glasses.

"What's the hat for?"

"For kicks."

"It's supposed to kind of tell us who you are?"

"You got it, bro. You're battin' a thousand."

"The hat'll have to go too."

"If you say so, bro."

He takes off the hat to reveal a Mohawk, dyed purple.

"Jesus Christ!" says Duke.

Angel laughs. "Jack in the box! Pop goes the weasel!"

"Maybe you want me to put it back on?"

"How are you feeling right now?" says Ray.

"Groovy. You're all the coolest. Far out. This is my kind of place."

"When a new member joins the group, we ask him to share an early childhood memory, a little bit about his life, how he got here. Are you willing to do that?"

"Anything you say, bro. Joey's here to please."

Joey bends over, looking at the floor, pondering, then straightens up and says "Early memory, huh? But maybe it's like the hat; maybe you don't really want to see what's under there."

"There are no secrets here."

"Whatever you say, bro."

As he talks, he drifts, as if he has taken a drug. "What I most remember is a drive-in movie. Not the movie. I was in the backseat. My mom and some guy took me. And I was about to float on off to sleep. When I hear somethin' funny. I heard 'em up there in the front seat gruntin' and smackin'. I didn't know what it was then, but they was fuckin' up there, bro. I shit you not. Bare-ass naked fuckin'."

"How did that make you feel?"

"Well. I was scared shitless. I was ashamed. I wanted to scream. I wanted to disappear into the seat covers. I wanted to die. Anything to be outta there."

He looks around and laughs.

Ray says, "Is it really funny to you?"

"Funnier than shit. One big fuckin' joke. My old lady was a junkie. When I was twelve, she tied off my arm and shot me up. Ya dig that? Mom and me used ta shoot up together. But I guess you've heard it all. No big deal. Just another of the eight million stories in the 'Naked City'. Right, bro? I don't even wanna think about all the other shit. But when I was fourteen, I split. 'Fuck *this* shit,' I said. I walked away. Hit the fuckin' streets."

"'Walked away,'" Rays says. "Heard that before. But can't get away. It always follows, no escape, it walks right along with us. You still used the drugs, I'm sure."

"Fuck, yes. Anything I could get my hands on."

"How did you live?"

"With my mouth and my ass."

"Do you want to talk about that?"

"Whatever you want."

"What do *you* want, Joe?"

"Me? Nothin'. And it's Joey."

"How old are you?"

"Thirty-eight."

"Jesus!" Duke snorts.

"His very self," Joey says.

Ray says, "That's not what Duke meant. You look more like twenty-four."

"Right on, bro. That's why the johns like me. Babyface. Angel face."

"Shit," says Angel.

"What's with her?" Joey asks Ray.

"That's her name. Angel."

"Wow! You my sister?"

"None other, darlin'. That's me..."

Ray interrupts. "You call yourself Joey?"

"I certainly do."

"Why?"

"Why? Shit, that's my name."

"I'd like to call you Joe."

"Whatever you want, bro. Suit your very self."

"And I'd like the group to call you Joe."

"Whatever, bro, Joey's just here to please."

"Joe," says Ray.

"Yeah, Joe then."

Another of those awkward pauses settles over the group. As usual, Ray lets it stew, almost never himself breaking it, but carefully watching who does—who it is that can't bear the continuing silence this particular time and what that might mean.

"Is it dump time?" Joe asks.

Ray says nothing.

"You know, feedback. I've been in these groups before. I talked. Now it's time for all of you to dump your shit all over my head, right?"

Laughter circles the group, but Ray is annoyed. "Is that what you think this is all about?" he asks Joe.

"No doubt in my mind."

"Then we're not going to do it." Looking around at the others, he asks, "So who else is ready to work?"

"Wait a minute," says Joe.

Ray waits for Joe.

"I *would* like to hear from my sister over there."

"Okay…Angel," Ray says, inviting her to talk.

"Yeah," she says, "Joey—Joe. I just want you to know that I know where you live."

"You live there too?"

"A lot of the time, yeah."

"Where is that?" Ray asks.

"Cloud cuckoo land," says Maggie.

"Fuck you, Maggie," says Angel.

"Where *do* you live, Angel?" Ray asks. "Joe, this is Angel Day."

"Wow!" Joe says, losing his cool, revealing himself—he is one of her worshipers.

Angel's eyes jump in anger. "I thought last names weren't supposed to be mentioned."

"Angel Day," Ray says. "Millions of albums sold. World tours. What is it they bill you as? 'The wild child.' The little girl every man wants to love. Is that you, Angel? Really?"

"That's little old me."

"Maggie really bothers you, doesn't she?"

"I don't pay her any attention at all."

"I think you do."

"She thinks I'm just a cunt."

"How's that make you feel?"

"Angry."

"But the anger's just a defense, isn't it? The anger covers something else, doesn't it?"

"I don't know. I just know what she says can't touch me."

"You think nobody can touch you, right?"

"You reach me sometimes."

"You don't even know what you feel, do you?"

"I know I feel afraid sometimes…"

Ray interrupts. "Can't be. Not the wild child, Angel Day."

"I don't know why," she says. "Sometimes at the concerts, or at the airports, when they're screaming and clawing at me, I get a little scared. Well, sometimes real scared. If they could get at me, they might actually tear me to pieces. Devour me. Make me them. But what Maggie thinks, that's just wrong. Read the stories on me, Maggie. They called me 'the Emily Dickinson of rock and roll.' I quote, Maggie: 'Her lyrics are poetry. The music is as complex as rock can be. Rock has found its Bach, with the face of an angel and the body of a succubus.' I created Angel Day. Nobody else did. The words, the music, the choreography, the whole God-damn show. They called it one of the most stunning rock performances ever. 'She makes Mick Jagger look like a harmless and foolish little elf.' That's what they said, Maggie."

"But then there's the booze and the cocaine," says Ray. "They say your voice is in trouble, that your vocal cords are burning out."

"Bullshit. And so what? That just gives me timbre, an edge, a little howl, a little moan, some miles of bad road. Makes them want me even more."

"Until it goes completely."

"Who cares? I've got enough money to take care of everybody in this room for the rest of their lives."

"I'm available for adoption, babe," says Duke.

"Me too," says Joe.

Alex and Paula laugh. Even Ray laughs.

Ray says, "Is that what's going to save you? The money?"

There is a long silence as she ponders this, then says, as if announcing a final, non-appealable verdict, "No."

"And the cocaine? Tell us about that."

"I stopped snorting it when my nose started to go bad."

"But started shooting it."

"Yeah. Right again."

"And then there's the heroin."

"How'd you know about that?"

"What difference does it make? The point is, I know. Another secret you don't have to conceal anymore."

"Well, I give you credit. You've done your God-damn homework."

"And all those canceled concerts. Angel Day, the 'No Show.' When was your last album? More than two years ago. When was the last time you finished a song, Angel?"

"Stop it."

"The jig's up, isn't it, Angel? You're disappearing right before our eyes. 'No show.'"

"That's mean. Problem is, I love that needle too much. The whole trip." She drifts into a reverie..."I tie up my arm tight. Tight as hell. Pain! It wants to explode. The needle penetrates the vein. A coldness then. Like a muffled blow. An iron bar wrapped in a towel. But behind it is all the pain in the world. But then the pain turns to something else. I watch the needle fill the vein. I leave it sit there for a minute. I get a little light-headed just from feeling the needle. The steel in the skin. Then I draw out a little blood into the syringe... I'm a booter."

"And tell us what that means," Ray says.

"You draw the blood out. So your blood mixes with the coke in the syringe. It's called bootin'. And then I shoot. I fuck myself. Five little seconds and then the rush. It's the only thing better than comin'."

"And then what happens?"

"I fly. And it all goes away."

"What goes away?"

"The nothins. The fuckin' nothins."

"Are you ready to do some work now? Are you ready to tell us your secrets, tell us who you really are?"

"Nothin'. That's the secret. Nothin'. I was nothin'. Just a rich little bitch. I got anything I wanted and did anything I wanted. Big fuckin' deal. My parents...parents, my ass. *They* were the children. Drank a ton, smoked grass, snorted coke. No needles for them. But if it was new, they did it. Every head-shrinker fad they glommed onto. Human potential, that's what they were into. Human potential, my ass. Liberals too they were...'social' ones anyway. I had a party my sophomore year in high school, and they served white wine!

"I don't know what happened to me. I guess I just looked around one day and said, this is shit, this is nothin'. I got to drinkin' and smokin' grass and poppin' pills. It just came with the territory.

"And all of us got into sex pretty early too. No big deal. It just went along with everything else. Shit, my dad's dirty friends were pawing at me by the time I was twelve. Old goat fuckers. I only made that mistake once, let one of those old goat fuckers get to me. I was fifteen. Dirty. I never felt so dirty. I wanted to die. Yeah, they're fuckin' children out there. They're taking away their childhoods so they can fuck 'em. That's what growin' up too fast is all about…"

Interrupting, Ray turns to Paula. "What about that, Paula? How does that make you feel?" Paula just shakes her head in refusal.

Angel, puzzled, glances inquisitively at Ray and Paula but then resumes, first taking a deep breath, as if steeling herself for what is coming. "And I don't know when this started—in high school, maybe earlier, but I kept thinkin' about dyin'. Not really on purpose. Just by takin' a little too much. Just seein' how far away I could float, and if I floated away forever, that was okay too. Nothin' to nothin'. I didn't have the music in me then. Not until later. And when I was a senior in high school, I was in my room. I had the guest house, separate from the main house. They never bothered me out there. They would never come down there without callin' first. I was real down that day, or up, whatever it was. Just thinkin' about fading on out of here. Goodbye, motherfuckers. And I started smokin' some grass, one joint after another. Good stuff. I had pills too, enough to float on away for good. And I was really ready. I took all the pills and almost did it. My parents didn't find me. The fucking maid found me. And somewhere there, when I was floatin' out there, I thought, hey, girl, fuck it, you might as well live. So I walked right up to death…and then I just walked away… And after it was over, I spent some time away, in the funny farm, and I'll be damned if the music didn't come into me then. And the rest is the Angel Day story. Read the articles if you want to know about her."

"So," Ray says, "here sits the child of a world that has nothing left but its dazzling corruption to hide its emptiness from itself. She tried to fill up the emptiness that was her only birthright by making herself an object of desire. And there will always be takers. The users. Just like those screaming crowds that want to worship and devour you."

She hunches over, stares at the ground, scoots up to the edge of her chair. "Sometimes when I'm up there on that stage, I'm lookin' at their eyes. And I think, Okay, motherfuckers. *Pant. Pant.* Those eyes. All of them. Boys. Girls. Hunger. Want. They want what I've got. Which is exactly nothin'. But they don't even know that.

"And now the music's dying, isn't it?"

"It was, but I'm feeling it again now."

"You're sober and clean now."

"Clean? I'm not clean. No drugs, but I'm not clean."

"You still want to die, Angel?"

"Not enough to do it."

"What's keeping you alive?"

"I don't know. Maybe the music. Maybe the glory."

"And the drugs are killing the music. And the glory's never enough."

"Fuck it."

"But you can't stop taking the drugs. Because the music and the glory aren't enough. Trapped."

"Fuck it."

"Stop searching, Angel, you're already home."

She shrugs.

"That was great work. Are you willing to hear the group's reactions?"

"Sure," she says, unsure.

"Okay. Duke?"

Duke fidgets, shakes his head, leans back in his chair as if warding off a blow. "Shit, I don't know. God damn it, Angel, I don't know what to say. What's wrong with you? You got every fuckin' thing...I don't know. This shit's a mystery to me."

Joe says, "Hey, sister. I know. You know I know. Okay?"

"Fuckin-A, Joe."

"Anyone else? Maggie?"

"Really? You really want to hear from me on this, Ray?

Ray says nothing.

"Okay then…You're valuable, Angel. Because you show them who they really are. I could almost feel the dicks get hard in here. That's all they are. You're not good for much else, but you're the best there is for that."

"Shit," says Duke. "It's funny you say that, Maggie, because I'd have sworn I saw *your* dick gettin' real hard over there."

"Duke," Ray says, "one more time and you're out of this group, and, as far as I'm concerned, out of this place. The next thing you'll see is your parole officer. And, Maggie, just judgments. Cruel judgments. That's all those are. What did you *feel* when you heard Angel's story?"

"Who cares? Joy maybe."

"And how does that make *you* feel, Angel? You're dying and Maggie feels joy. That's what happens to symbols, Angel."

"Fuck her. She can't touch me. None of them can touch me."

"They've got their hands all over you."

He looks around the group. "Anyone else? Alex, this woman needs us. Desperately needs us, whether she believes so or not. She needs gifts. Can you give her one?"

"Okay," says Alex, "I guess I'm just one of those hard dicks. I felt that. No big deal. Just something to get out of the way first. Such an ugly story. But there's something false in that story. Like a red herring. Something else comes out in the music. It's not all fuck music. There's a whole other thing. A lifting up."

"Dumb luck," says Angel, "pure coincidence."

"Angel," Ray says, "I hear you say that, and it just makes me sick and sad. It's not dumb luck. It's not coincidence. It's you. The real you. Alex is telling you who you really are. But you don't want that. Instead, you settle for whatever you think your worshipers tell you to be. You say you created Angel Day. Not so. *They* created Angel Day. Do you really hate yourself that much? Or is it because they won't pay for the real thing, they won't worship the real thing? You hate them for it, but what chance have you ever given them? Why don't you give them something better than they're asking for? What's *your* responsibility? Why don't *you* begin it, Angel?"

Angel leans back in her chair, lifts her head, looks toward the ceiling. Silence descends again, and this time Ray himself breaks it. "I'm wondering what others are feeling right now."

Duke is greatly agitated and speaks directly to Ray. "I'm feeling God-damned pissed off, that's what I'm feelin'. It's just gibberish." He speaks directly to Ray. "All this is just gibberish. I'm tired of it. You people are all nuts. You got the whole world turned upside down. You fuck with the normal people in here and kiss the asses of all the perverts."

"Watch it, Duke," Ray warns.

"I thought it was all about 'rigorous honesty,' Mr. Counselor. Well, here it is. If I get one inch out of line, you threaten to kick me out. And you know what that means for me, the slammer. I lose my job, my retirement. I lose everything. But fuck that. You don't care about that. Fuck workin' for a living. That's just shit to you people. Everything normal is just shit to you people. I mean you let the faggots prance around here like they own the fuckin' place, which, for all I know, they do."

He looks around, wanting to provoke. "And you just look the other way when those two," pointing to Maggie and Paula, "are touchin' and huggin' and feelin' each other right in front of everybody."

Paula leaps up from her chair and screams, "You vicious man! You vicious bastard!"

6

RAY, SURPRISED BY Paula's outburst because it is so out of her character, is confused for a moment. Recovering, he says, "Okay, Paula, no name calling. Just tell him how he makes you feel."

"He's so vicious. As if affection is a sin."

Maggie says, "If he can't fuck it, he tries to kill it."

"We haven't done anything like that," Paula says.

"You're losing it, Paula," says Ray. "He's winning."

"He makes me ashamed. He just makes me want to crawl off and die."

"Like your father, Paula?"

"My father wasn't like him." She sobs. "My father was gentle..."

"Your father was evil."

"You're wrong! You don't understand!"

"Evil, Paula. The father of lies."

"No..."

"Worse than Duke, Paula. Worse than Duke by far."

"Then I'm evil too."

"That's exactly what he wants you to believe. It's time to deal with him. He's dead, but his hands are still on you."

"You can't tell them."

"No more secrets, Paula. There's no more time for secrets. The secrets are killing you even more than the pills are killing you. I'll help you. The group will help you. This may be your last chance, Paula."

Maggie begs, "Do it, Paula, please."

Angel says, "We love you, Paula."

"I can't!" Paula cries out.

Ray stands up and signals to Maggie to switch chairs with him so that he is sitting next to Paula.

"Alex, get the batacca please."

Alex rises from his chair, goes to the wall where the batacca rests, picks up the bat, slides the cushion over in front of Paula, then stands holding the bat out to her.

She hesitates.

"You have to talk to him," says Ray, not commanding now, imploring. "You have to tell him what he did to you. The shame. The shame you turn on yourself. Give it back to him. It's not yours. It's his."

She takes the batacca from Alex.

Ray points to Duke. "There he is. Talk to him."

"Not him."

"Yes, him. It's him. Think of Duke as your father. Tell him what it's really like for you, Paula. Duke, move up here closer."

"Fuck this," says Duke, "I'm not gonna do it."

"Do it! Move up here now! For once you're gonna help someone."

Angel and Alex visibly squirm, an involuntary almost unconscious response to the vehemence of Ray's rage at Duke. They sense Ray is nearly unhinged, has arrived at some breaking point.

"Don't make him do that, Ray," Angel says, "it's not right."

"Shut up, Angel," Ray says, nearly shouting. "You're not helping. Duke, are you going to do what I say or not?"

Duke moves his chair slightly forward, only minimally complying.

"Talk to him, Paula," Ray commands.

She takes in a deep breath, and her voice quivers with emotion. "Daddy...She stops. "Ray, I can't do this! I can't look at *him*," pointing to Duke.

Thwarted, Ray gives up on this angle. "Okay, Paula. Move back, Duke."

"Thank God!" says Angel.

Duke gets up, leaving the empty chair in front of Paula, and returns to his seat. But he is still not far away from Paula and is directly in her line of sight.

"Okay, Paula," says Ray, gentle again. "No more excuses, no more evasions. It's time. Do it right now. Please, Paula. Trust me. I know what you need. Talk to the chair like *he's* in it."

She takes a few moments to gather herself, then says, "Daddy...I know Mother was so cold..."

"Paula!" Ray interrupts. "Don't start blaming your mother. That's what he wants you to do. Look at him. Look him right in the eyes. Now bang that thing. Bang it hard just once, and it will all come out, I promise. *Bang it!*"

She slowly raises the batacca over her head, gathers her strength, and brings it down surprisingly hard against the cushion, making a loud *whack!*

She speaks slowly, intermittently pounding the batacca.

"The baths is where it started."

Whack! The vehemence of it makes Ray and several others flinch.

"You used to give me the baths. You rubbed me with the washcloth. All over."

Whack!

"You said, 'Do you want to play like you're Mommy?'...And it did feel good."

Whack!

"God help me Daddy, it did feel good," she says, her voice reaching a higher pitch, almost breaking. "Why did you make it feel so good?"

She pounds the batacca even harder than before. *Whack!*

Ray, in almost a whisper, asks, "And then what?"

"You came into my room…night after night."

Whack!

"And then what, Paula?"

"You died, Daddy."

"Tell him what your life has been like, Paula."

"Terrible. It's been terrible, Daddy."

Whack!

"Tell him how old you are now, Paula."

"Thirty-five, Daddy."

"Tell him how many times you've been married."

"Four times, Daddy."

Whack!

"Tell him what they did to you."

"They weren't nice. They beat me up. They beat me up bad."

"Time after time. But you never left them, did you, Paula?"

Whack!

"They left me, Daddy. You were the only one in the world that wanted me."

Whack! "They hated me. They beat me." She smashes it again—*Whack!*—and screams, "They beat me to a pulp!"

Whack!

"And did you deserve that?" Ray asks.

She falters. "I guess I did…"

Ray loses control. His voice becomes high-pitched. "Oh no you didn't. Don't look at me! Look at him! Nobody deserves that. Especially a little girl whose only mistake was to trust her father. Look at him, Paula."

"And *she* knew, Daddy. She knew!" *Whack!*"

"You were the only child. Mother's gift to Daddy."

Whack! "Witch!"

"What about *him*? Why aren't you angry at *him*?"

"I loved him."

"Tell him that, Paula."

"I love you, Daddy." She is sobbing so much she can hardly speak. "Oh God, I'm so ashamed!"

"Tell him what shame feels like, Paula."

"I'm a worm, Daddy," she says, without self-pity, harsh, a verdict, merciless. "A slimy, fat worm."

"Were you always a worm, Paula?"

"I really was a little girl once."

"But," Ray says very softly, "he stole the little girl from her crib and put a worm in her place."

Whack!

"Yes…Daddy, that's what you did."

She is sobbing now, taking in great gulps of breath.

"But you're not angry at *him*?"

"I don't know…"

Disgusted, almost giving up, Ray says, "That's it. Good old Paula. Let him off the hook."

Paula, trancelike, says, "Just a worm, wriggling on the hook."

Whack!

"Tell him how much you hate yourself. Tell him about the pills… all those pills."

Half-heartedly obliging, she says, "I hate myself, Daddy."

"Scream it, Paula! Shout it from the rooftops! Scream it!"

Whack! She screams, "*I hate myself!*"

Whack!

Silence falls, broken, finally, by Paula.

"I can't stand it anymore. Daddy, I am thinking that…you…made me the worm."

"That's right, Paula," Ray says, his voice again very soft, no anger anymore, a husky voice full of love and pain. "That's what he did. How could he do that to a helpless little girl?"

Whack!

Across from Paula, Duke is agitated, squirming.

Whack! Paula screams, "You're the worm, Daddy*!*"

Whack!

She is becoming exhausted, and in this last effort she exerts all of her remaining strength. "You worm! You—*Whack!*— Slimy—*Whack!* —Worm!..."

Duke has been growing more and more agitated and now suddenly breaks down, sobbing, shocking all the others, who gape and look on.

Ray tries to ignore Duke and keep the focus on Paula. "Give him back the shame now, Paula. It's his, not yours."

Duke jumps up. "Stop! Please stop! God-damn it, stop!"

Paula is amazed, sinking and fading. "He's crying. I hurt him."

"Damn it," Ray says. "He's winning again, Paula."

"But he's crying. Duke's crying."

"He won. He hooked you with his tears. What the hell is going on with you, Duke?"

Duke collapses back down on his chair. "I'm sorry!" he yells, near hysteria. "I'm sorry!"

"Oh God, Duke," Ray says. "Do you have a secret too?"

"I did that." He points to Paula. "To my daughter."

Ray lurches forward in his chair as if he might physically attack Duke. "And now you want to say you're sorry?"

"I do. I do."

"Well, fuck you, Duke. We don't accept your apology."

Alex, shocked, lurches toward the edge of his chair, on the verge of jumping up from it. "What are you saying?"

Ray ignores him. He has become a dark, avenging angel. "And what is she going through out there on those nasty fucking streets because of you, Duke? And you weep, you miserable son of a bitch, and beg for our sympathy."

"Ray!" Angel cries out as the others squirm.

Ray will not relent. "You cry, and Paula dies."

"Stop it!" says Angel.

"You come in here every day and foul the room with your bigotry, your cruelty, your hatred, your fake macho bullshit, your stinking fear. Normal! Is that what you called yourself just a little while ago? Look around you, Duke." Ray's hand makes a circle around the group. "There they are. Your creations. They keep coming in here, Duke. Your victims. Day after day, year after year. They're lined up out there, and the line is getting longer all the time. All over the world, Duke. And they'll stay lined up out there forever. I'm sick to death of your victims, Duke."

"What're you saying, man?" cries Alex.

But Ray persists. "And now, Duke, you want to go and die on us, isn't that right? You want to go and die on us and leave us alone with the harm you've done us."

Alex leaps up from his chair as if he is about to attack Ray physically. Angel yells, "Ray, God-damn it, *stop!*"

This finally stops him. He looks around, startled, as if he has just awakened abruptly from a deep sleep and doesn't know where he is. "Oh God," he says, leans back and sits bolt upright in his chair, then collapses, bends over, puts his face in his hands for many seconds as the group members look helplessly at each other, wondering what has happened, what they should do, who they should comfort and how.

Finally, he drops his hands and raises himself up. "Oh, Duke!" he says. I'm so sorry…so sorry. All of you. So sorry. What am I doing?"

He pauses as he recovers and gathers himself, struggling to become the old masterful Ray again. "Duke, please believe me, I am sorry from the bottom of my soul… But we can't lose this moment. We can't lose it because of me, because I did that. We have to go on."

He has recovered now. "What's it like to be unforgiven, Duke? You've got another secret, don't you? Except this secret I know. The doctor told me. What did you find out last week? You haven't told us what you found out last week."

"Who gives a *shit* about that?"

"Oh, we do, Duke. *I* do. Tell us, Duke."

"I'm a dead man. Leukemia. No more than a year. So what. My just desserts."

"But to die unforgiven."

"Oh, God!"

"Do you believe in God, Duke?"

Duke nods his head. "Yes."

"Does your God forgive?"

"I don't know."

"Do you want forgiveness?"

"I do," he says loudly, his voice breaking, "more than anything!"

"Then ask."

"She's not here. I don't know where she is."

"Ask."

"*Forgive me!*"

"I forgive you, Duke," says Ray as he kneels down in front of Duke and grabs Duke's hands. "I forgive you."

"You're not God. You're not her."

"But I'm all you've got right now."

Angel leaves her chair and kneels on the floor beside Duke and puts her hands on his arm and says, "Not *all*. I forgive you, Duke."

Alex and Joe also move to Duke and kneel on the floor beside him.

"Not *all*," Alex says. "I forgive you, Duke."

"Jesus, man," says Joe. "I forgive you too. Let it go, man. Give it up."

"These victims forgive you, Duke," Ray says. He looks around. "Maggie?"

She shakes her head. "No. I can't. I won't. This is just another cheap stunt, Ray."

"I forgive," says Paula.

"Not yet, Paula," Ray says. "You're not ready yet."

Ray stands and moves back to his chair. Angel, Alex, and Joe follow. Ray turns again to Duke. "Duke, when you get out of here, you've got to try and find her somehow. If you don't find her, that's okay. The search will be enough. But if you do find her, just say you're sorry and ask for forgiveness. If you can do something more, do it, but above all do that. There's nothing else you can do now. And while you're searching, Duke, you'll have to find a way to forgive yourself."

"Never."

"Do you know what hell is, Duke? The unforgiven. Don't consign yourself to hell. Can you pray?"

"I think so."

"Then pray for the courage to find her and ask her, and if you can't or she won't, look it right in the face, right in the mirror, and forgive yourself. Say to yourself, 'I was that man, but I am no longer that man, and I will do whatever I can to make reparation. I will earn my forgiveness by making reparation.' And then carry the message. Just a little bit. If only to just another victim or two. You've been a fool and a coward a lot of your life, but that will be the bravest thing you could ever do. Will you do that? It's called redemption."

"I will try."

"No, Duke, you *will.*"

"I will."

Ray looks at his watch. "We're overtime. We have to stop."

Alex, Joe, and Angel return to their seats. Ray sits quietly for a while, lost in himself, as the others wait in dread for him to return to them.

He lifts his head. "I guess it's time to quit. What have I forgotten? I've forgotten something…Paula…that's what I forgot. I can't forget you. All your life we've been forgetting you."

"I'm here," says Paula.

"So, do you know the gospel story about the light under the bushel basket?"

"I do."

"We saw your light today. It was beautiful. Terrible. But beautiful too. You lifted the bushel, just for a minute. That's not your basket. They put it over you. You were just a little girl, and they shrouded you in darkness. Your light could hardly be seen. Just a dim ray. But it was there. It was still there. What you didn't know, for all these years, is that you can lift up that shroud. That little girl was waiting for Daddy to lift it up. But he won't lift it. He wants it to stay there so he won't be seen. That little girl who was in the light and then was shrouded in darkness, only she can lift it up. And only if you let her, the child inside you. She wants to, Paula. I know that."

"She does," Paula says. She is so exhausted she can barely speak. "I know she does. I want to live. I really do."

All are quiet for several seconds. Then Angel begins to sing in a high, clear, calm voice the old spiritual. Not a gospel shout. It is 'little', like the light itself, a slow and quiet, almost shy rendition.

This little light of mine,

I'm gonna let it shine.

This little light of mi—ine,

I'm gonna let it shine.

Let it shine,

Let it shine,

Let it shine.

As she continues to sing, the others, one by one, somewhat awkwardly join her. Joe, then Alex, then Paula, and finally, even Duke. The ascending chorale rises in layers, but Angel maintains control, adjusting to and enhancing the others' voices as they enter, in full charge of the tempo, keeping it measured, composed. She manages a centered stillness, lifting her voice, effortlessly and unhurried, octave by octave, always reaching slightly above the others. For all of them, the song becomes a prayer. Only Maggie and Ray do not join in.

All through the night,

I'm gonna let it shine.

All through the ni—ight,

I'm gonna let it shine.

Let it shine,

Let it shine,

Let it shine.

Ray, his face all pain, moves to the window, his back to the group. He looks out and upward.

"Everywhere I go,

I'm gonna let it shine.

Everywhere I go-o,

I'm gonna let it shine.

Let it shine…

On the last two lines, Angel's voice soars far above the others.

Let it shine,

Let it shine.

The group looks at Ray's back. He does not move, says nothing. They stare uncertainly. Finally, they realize they just need to leave. Angel and Alex hug Paula. Maggie and Paula leave. Alex, Joe, and Angel hug Duke. Duke, Joe, and Alex leave together. Angel and Ray remain. Ray still looks out the window, Angel watching him.

"What's goin' on over there? What're you lookin' for out there?"

He still does not turn around but talks to the window and something out there. "Moths and flames. Rainbows and pots of gold. I can't stand it anymore. It's time to get on that raft again and float on down the river."

"Well then, call me Jim. But I can't figure you. Duke. Paula. You went off the deep end there for a minute, but what a recovery, man. The forgiveness thing. The light and the bushel thing. That was beautiful. So what's wrong?"

Ray leaves the window and sits down wearily at his desk. "I can still talk the talk, but I can't walk the walk anymore. Spells. Incantations. Words to live by. Mirrors. Illusions. Ray's magic show. Stunts, just like Maggie said. I reach into my bag of tricks and pull out one for each of them. Does Duke believe in God? Yes? Then I offer him forgiveness. Is Paula a Christian? Yes? Then I give her a Bible story. I find the words they will hear, and I say those words to them. "Here, you poor junkie, take these words. Grab onto these words of mine, these fictions, this bullshit of mine that I don't even believe anymore, and maybe you'll be able to live somehow. Here. Take this pretty wool I've woven and pull it over your eyes. So you won't see what's going on out there. All the victims. Millions of them. All over the earth. For everyone who's saved in here, there's a thousand being made out there. You said it. The fucking of the children. And Alex...'the babies in the frying pans.'"

"Is *that* your problem, Ray? You want to save them all? All the babies...?"

"All. All or none."

"'The things I cannot change,' Ray. Remember that? The things *you* cannot change. I keep wonderin' why you wanna carry everybody else's cross. Didn't ya hear the news? Christ's already been here."

"It really is just a game. Like you say, Angel—dumb luck, pure coincidence. Just a game. Ray's game. God's game. Darwin's game. Whoever's fucking game it is, I don't want to play it anymore. I want refuge. I want the green light...the pot of gold."

7

. . . A G A I N, RAY GESTURES toward the whiteboard. "Primary and progressive. And chronic. Incurable. Remission, yes. Cure, no. Only death will cure you. Like me, you tried to medicate the pain with the drugs, and for a while it seemed to work. But then it only made things worse. It turned you into a monster. So you grieve. You need to do that. Right here in this place. Grieve for the monster that frees you from pain, then eats you alive, the monster you love. Grieve, then let it die. Let it go. For God's sake, let it go. If you let the monster go, everything else is possible. Even hope is possible. It's easy for me to describe the despair of addiction. It's harder for me to describe the simple joys of recovery. But go to the meetings. Listen to the stories. That's where you'll find your strength. In the stories. People brought back from the dead. Miracles everywhere. You don't have to believe in God to believe in miracles. A miracle is simply an inexplicable change for the better. Those of you who believe in God, a just God, you're already halfway there. The rest of you...of us...I don't know. Long ago we threw away God and eternal life, sort of traded hope in God for hope in Man. And now that hope's dead too. We live in the absurd universe now. But you've got to find comfort somewhere. Grab it, wherever you can find it.

Most addicts don't make it. Experts say that something like eighty-five percent of us die in our disease. Even you fortunate ones who somehow managed to get here—where you've got a better chance—a third of you, maybe half of you, maybe more, won't make it. Why? Why you and not the other guy? Why the other guy and not you? I don't know. Everybody's got an answer. There are a million answers. And none of them make any sense. It drives me crazy.

And those of you who aren't going to make it, who will go out of here and die in their disease, I wish you wouldn't, but I know you will. I know you will, and I can't stand it. And to be honest, rigorously honest, I don't think I'm gonna make it either. I can't find a refuge. The flames. We weren't made for the flames. We were made to lie down in green pastures. I wish I could believe that. I wish I could believe anything. I can't accept all the pain, the random cruelty, the fucking of the children, the babies in the frying pans. They say Satan rebelled from Pride. I don't believe that. Satan rebelled because God would not reveal himself. Satan was condemned to everlasting torment because he tried to rip the mask from the inscrutable face of God.

There's only one way. One day at a time for the rest of your life. This is a physical disease, but the only cure for it is spiritual. We have to heal our wounds, or bandage them if we can't heal them. Starting right here in this place. Because if we don't heal them, someday we'll want that little lift, and we'll reach for the drug, and then the disease will take over. *We* can't heal you. The best we can do is show you something in yourselves and others, some wellspring of goodness, of decency, of won-der--some gentle, quiet, mysterious thing inside you. Some will find it, some won't. That's just the way it is. Because of this curse that afflicts us, we have to live on a higher spiritual plane. Just to stay alive we have to embrace this insane universe. And love it somehow. Love it with all our might. Embrace the universe. Without reservation. Without reservation!

I don't know. I don't know at all. Don't listen to me anymore. I've got nothing left to say. Only this—a poem. A haiku. Japanese. Twelve words. Issa was the poet's name. His child died. And he wrote this:

> This dewdrop world
> It may be a dewdrop
> And yet—and yet

And yet. And yet. The saddest words in all the world. Forget those yets! You're dewdrops! Dewdrops! And there's only one thing in the world for you to do. Glisten. And forget those yets. Forget them!

8

PETER SITS BEHIND Ray's desk in Ray's office, the telephone to his ear. "Let me talk to Mr. Lord."

The woman on the other end of the line asks, "May I tell him what it's about?"

"No, you may not tell him what it's about. Quit screwing me around and let me talk to him."

He waits, drumming his fingers on the desk.

Lord comes on the line. "Hello, Peter, I hear you're upset."

"I've got some very bad news. I wanted to report it to you directly. I lost a counselor. My best."

"I have a feeling I know who that is."

"Yes, it's Ray. He's drunk. He called in. I'm clearing his desk out right now. And there's more. Angel Day took off last night."

"Shit. Why didn't someone talk her out of it?"

"Nobody even knew she was gone until this morning. Left most of her stuff here. And there's more. And worse. I think she went after Ray."

"I can see the God damn headlines now."

"Yes. Bad. The worst. That's why I thought you should know right away. Maybe you can talk to her press people. Maybe we can keep it contained somehow."

"Who knows about it?"

"Well, I've already told the patients. I talked to the whole community a few minutes ago. The place is a madhouse. Half of them are trying to leave."

"That was a dumb fucking thing to do, Peter."

"Well, maybe it was a mistake. But I don't really think so. Rigorous honesty, remember? If we don't live by our principles, how can we expect the patients to? 'Let it begin with me.'"

"Don't spout that crap at me. This is existential, you idiot. This could wipe us out. You're supposed to be my rock solid leader, Peter, and you've *panicked*...fucked us good."

"Well, I'll tell you this, Mr. Lord. If you don't like the way I'm doing this job, you can take it *and shove it up your ass!*"

He slams down the phone. Near tears, he curses to the empty room, "God *damn* it, Ray!"

9

RAY SITS IN darkness at a wooden table in the front room of his apartment. He drinks a large shot glass empty, then refills it from a half-full bottle of *Wild Turkey* sitting on the table. A pitcher of water and a pitcher of ice sit next to the whiskey bottle. The table separates the kitchen behind it from the living room in front of it. Similar art pieces to those in his office hang on the walls. As in his office, a large print of Homer's *Gulfstream* broods over the room. Bookshelves cover the walls where no art pieces hang, stuffed with books, just like the bookshelves in his office. The other furniture is sparse, unremarkable. The place is not without comfort, but it is not comfortable.

From a stereo speaker mounted on a wall, Angel's music plays, one of her most famous songs, "The Night You Brought Me Home."

I was bored, adrift, alone.

You were baffled and so shy,

Solemn face but smiling eyes.

Miracles always take us by surprise.

The night you brought me home…

It is one of her more gentle songs, not like the driving, blazing anthems charged with eroticism that she is so famous for, but something softer.

That moon and my hopes surged into the sky.

That moon was drunk like you and I,

But still we took our chance.

"Yes," I said, "let's dance."

The night you brought me home...

The song moves briskly forward, thoughtful but not slow, pulsating always, in no hurry but always driven by an insistent beat. That's what Angel understands deep in her bones and blood—that the beat is everything—all of it—all the sex, all the drugs, all the rock 'n roll.

Will we be lovers

Or just friends?

What can we make?

What can we do,

What be and become?

Are we awake or asleep?

Will our promises keep?

She oscillates high to low constantly and effortlessly. They call her the queen of vibrato. She has so fully explored and ultimately mastered her voice and its limits that she tricks her listeners into thinking she has no limits, that there is no note she cannot hit at will. She can hit all the high notes when she thinks she needs to, but her voice is mostly deep and rough, finding its truth exactly there, in that patch of briar rose. She is here to dazzle, not to soothe.

Silver shards of moonbeam

Promised us everything.

Fog pierced by lamppost lights

Roman candles bursting in the dark

The night you brought me home...

A solo saxophone riffs in and rises high in a long, insistent lament. She has learned that she can not only survive but even triumph by throwing away the formula from song to song or even within the same song. Most of all, she has learned that the best songs told stories.

Should we take our shot

Or just wonder why?
Do we dare to dream,
Are we only what we seem
The night you brought me home...

A violin plays the same riff as the saxophone.

But for just a moment I looked away.
My gaze wandered off somewhere.
And when I looked back,
You weren't there
The night you brought me home.

Ray pushes a button on the remote. The song starts again. He hears a knock on the door. He does not move. Another knock. He still does not move. The door opens. She is wearing sandals; a short black slip dress, her arms and shoulders bare; thin golden bracelets around each of her wrists; a small turquoise ring on her left ring finger, an amethyst on her right; large, thin hoop-like earrings; lilac-tinted sunglasses—a casual loveliness. She holds a bottle of wine in one hand, her purse in another.

"Hey, Dewdrop," she says.

"Go away."

"If *this,*" she says, waving the wine bottle at him, "is what you're worried about, I've already been there. The deed, my man, is already done."

Sadly he says, "Jesus, Angel."

She points at one of the stereo speakers mounted on the wall. "I felt you calling me. I really did. When you weren't there two days ago, when you weren't there yesterday, I knew. Right away, I knew."

She glides to the table. "How 'bout a glass?"

"Go away. Really. Go on."

"Come off the bullshit, darlin'. Didn't you hear me? I felt you calling me. You hear that? You were calling me."

"A dirty trick too. Who will forgive *me?*"

"Fuck that. I wasn't ready anyway. I've got some runnin' left to do."

"Some dying left to do."

"And some living too."

"You may never get back."

"Fuck it. I was born to die, wasn't I?"

She sets the wine bottle down, scooches up on the table, sits on it facing him, just to the right of him, swinging her legs a little. "Now, how 'bout that glass?"

Ray surrenders. "Ice?" he asks.

"A bit. Not much."

He rises and wearily retrieves a glass from a kitchen cabinet, returns to the table, and sets the glass down in front of him and next to her. He stands over her. They are as close as they can be without actually touching each other.

"Mind my hands?" he asks, as he lifts cubes out of the ice bucket. "The butler made off with the ice tongs."

"No, darlin', I won't mind your hands one bit."

He drops three cubes into her glass. "Water?"

"A touch."

He pours in a little water, hands the glass to her, and sits down. She pours a generous amount of whiskey. He picks up his glass, offers a silent toast. They touch their glasses softly together and drink.

She says, "Til death do us part. I wasn't wrong about one thing. I do love you. Do you love me?"

He takes a long time to answer. "Here's rigorous honesty. Even if we're capable of that now, we won't be for long."

"It's gonna be fine."

"Maybe. For a while."

"What else do you want? Like they say in AA, 'a day at a time.'" She laughs a little at her joke. Nodding her head toward the sound of her voice from the speaker, she says, "Pretty good music, huh? I've got some more in me."

"For a while maybe."

"God, Ray, give us a break. Let's do somethin' fun. Let's not waste this."

She moves off the table in a little jump, kicks off her sandals, turns to face him, and straddles his knees. She kisses him. He slides his hands up underneath her dress.

"It's time," she says.

"The first time is the worst time," he says.

"Not for us, babe," she says. "It's the night you brought me home."

Like the bridegrooms always do in the old movies, he sweeps her up in his arms and carries her across the living room and over the threshold of his bedroom.

"Hey, a futon," she says. "Perfect. Ray, the Buddhist monk."

"But it didn't quite turn out that way in the end," he says.

"Hey, we'll still put it to good use."

With her still in his arms he carefully descends to his knees on the futon and lays her down. Then he stands up, and she sits up. He slowly removes his clothes, and she removes hers. They both stare for a moment. She moves over, giving him room, and he kneels next to her and strokes her and kisses her with lips and tongue on her forehead and face and neck, and all up and down her. By the time she brings him inside her, she has already climaxed once, gently, with hardly more than a barely audible groan and then a litany of small sounds that one could mistake for pain but are, in fact, small cries of gratitude. He is ready now, and she is ready again. It happens quickly but lasts long. They could go on, but each knows that something nearly perfect has transpired, and they sense too that there is no reason to risk spoiling it by being greedy for more, these thoroughly immoderate creatures managing this one time to practice a wise moderation. They lie on their backs for a while, slightly apart, saying nothing. Then she rises to her knees, kisses the scars on his chest, and moves slowly down him.

This has sealed their covenant—and their fates—because this first time is exactly how they each imagined it could be. They are not so drunk that their senses are hopelessly numb—not so drunk they will fail to remember much, or any of it, the next morning—not coming together in a begrudging armistice, being the only means left for them to resolve, if only for the night, a drunken war of words or worse—not just fucking as a last resort because that is the only pleasure they are any longer able to extract from each other. No, this time is slow, quiet, and gentle—every movement, every gesture calculated to impart to the other pleasure most acute, persuading her especially, and even him, though he knows so much better, that whatever pain the future might bring will surely be worth this—this alone makes it worth it—and what reason is there to believe they cannot repeat this thing again and again? But even if they could manage to repeat it only one time more, they are deluded enough to believe that it is worth all the risk, all he danger, all the inevitable doom.

Later, they drift back to the table in the front room, she again straddling him, her arms around his neck, glass in hand. He is wearing only his jeans, she only his shirt.

"Maybe we should try to find that daughter of yours. I think I'd make a pretty good stepmom.

He laughs softly, knowing this is not her mockingbird self, she actually means it, and he will not, right now anyway, scoff at her dream. "You surely would," he says.

She slides off him, tosses down her drink and sits in the other chair. More to herself and the world than to him, she says, "Well, what do we do now?"

After a silence, she turns to him. "I still can't figure you out."

"I can't figure me either."

"Try. Help me. Who are you, Ray?"

He sets his glass down. "When I was a little boy, just eight or nine years old, my mother and one of those stepfathers of mine had one of their weekly brawls. But this time it was a little worse than usual. He pounded on her for a while, then left the house. I came downstairs, and she was sprawled on the couch, her lip split open and all puffed up, one eye swollen and almost closed. I got down on my knees in front of her, and I begged her, 'Mom, let's get out of here. Right now. Divorce him.' And she said, blubbering through her tears, 'I can't. I love him. I love him.' And without saying another word I got off my knees and went upstairs to my room. I didn't understand it until a long time later, but God died for me that night, and I knew from that time on I was alone. I sat in my pitch black bedroom looking out the window, up at the stars, and I vowed that from that moment I would turn my back on that world of insanity downstairs. I wished so much, I really did, to voyage to those stars and be lord of the universe, and from my kingdom in the stars reach down to the world, and I would banish pain. Of course I could do no such thing. But still, I think I've actually spent the rest of my life trying to keep that vow somehow, at least in the small part of the universe I've moved through. That's what the booze and the drugs were all about. That's what the counseling was all about. And I've tried to accept reality—the absurdity, the random cruelty, the senseless suffering, despair, and even death, eternal death, the final joke on us. But that little boy in that room, that little boy so full of hunger and so full of longing and want, that little boy would not grow up. He never changed. He just kept sitting there in that room, wanting. And despite all my words, all my tricks, I cannot make him change. He just keeps sitting there. His wound will not be healed. For him, it is everyone or no one at all. For him, it is all or nothing."

"And where do I fit into all that?"

"I was there, alone, my despair my only companion, the only companion I wanted. And you walked into the room. Wounded, but still so full of life. Sick unto death, but defiant still. With a different hunger but one as boundless and insatiable as my own. A garden of earthly delights. Softness and danger. Ecstasy and doom. A slap in the face of the universe.

The promise of a victory so sweet I'd wager my soul just to taste it for an instant. All it costs me is the price of a one-way ticket on a kamikaze flight. That's what the little boy was waiting for all the time. Because he would banish pain."

She pulls back and puts her hands on his shoulders. "You've gotta drop this despair stuff, darlin'. I can't take it. I wanna soar. Yeah, maybe I'll crash, and burn. But I'm gonna enjoy the flight."

"Icarus," he says.

Confused, a bit irritated, she says, "I don't follow."

"Icarus. The boy who wanted to fly to the sun. And he did. With a pair of wings made from wax and feathers. Higher and higher…each wonderful upward thrust brought him closer to the dream—'I'm gonna touch the sun!' But his wings were only made of wax. And he was only human after all. The sun melted the wax, and he plummeted down. The descent was so much faster than the climb, but even the fall was probably wonderful for him. And he crashed into the sea. Obliterated. Just flecks of foam on the breaking wave."

"That's it, darlin'. Lover. Brother. You got it right again. That's my story. And why not? Why not go for the sun? You want me to be humble? What for? That's the dirtiest trick of all the dirty tricks of that malicious fucking trickster up there in the sky. 'Be humble,' they tell you. 'Accept your lot in life.' You are, you become, you are no more. That's it? Eternal death? The fuckin' nothins forever? And you want me to go quietly to that? Well, bullshit! Hear me, Ray. This is my swan song. This is my epitaph. I'm not goin' down easy. I'm gonna fly until I die. I'm goin' for that God-damn sun every day of my life. And yeah, I know the wax is meltin' all the time. I know it, so I'll just beat those wings a little faster, get the most from every surge. And when it all melts, well, fuck it, Ray, it was a good day to die. And I won't really be completely nothin' then. Because I didn't live and die like some anonymous little nothin' of a girl. Because memories of me will haunt their nights and days. Because they'll keep telling my story. They won't be able to help themselves. They'll remember that girl that went for the God-damn sun!"

She pulls her chair around next to him, sits down, takes a rolled-up hand towel from her purse and unrolls it to reveal two hypodermic needles half-filled with liquid, a small bottle of alcohol, a wad of cotton, and a large, very thick rubber band. She lifts his arm and lays it flat on the table, wraps his arm above the elbow with the rubber band, daubs his exposed vein with the alcohol-soaked cotton, and inserts the needle.

"Ready?"

He nods his head. She injects the cocaine, saying, "Thousand one, thousand two, thousand three, thousand four, thousand five."

His head lolls back as he experiences the rush.

She says, softly, "Score! That's all we want. That's all anybody wants. Score!"

She unwinds the band from his arm and wraps up her own.

"You want help?" he says.

Intent, all her attention on the needle and her arm, "No, darlin'. This is my trip. All mine."

Slowly, drawing out the vowel as she injects herself, "Sc-o-o-o-re."

He pours himself a drink, brings it to his lips but stops, for he is not much interested in such tame stuff now, and he sets the glass back down abruptly, spilling some of the liquor onto the table.

Mimicking her—the cocaine is taking over—he says, his voice something new, charged with excitement, "What's next, darlin'?"

"Mexico!" she says. "Dance by the sea in Mexico!"

"I have one better. Florida! My boat!"

"Yes! Sweet, sweet, sweet. Can we get my piano on that boat?"

"We can do anything."

"If not, we'll just buy a bigger fuckin' boat. I still got the music. You wanna be my manager?"

He does not respond. He is not paying attention.

"What's goin' on over there, Ray?"

"Fuck it, girl! We're gonna go for it! The sun, the flames, the pot of gold, the green light, everything! Why not? Why the fuck not?"

"Dewdrops," she says. "Glisten, darlin'. Glisten."

She takes the remote control and brings up the volume gradually until it roars. The song playing is the opposite, a virtual negation of "The Night You Brought Me Home." It's called "The Lies We Told" and includes not a single moment of respite. From the first note it leaps right at its listeners.

Those lies we told
Got us by,
Propped us up,
Let us fly.

Her voice summons again those stunning waves of vibrato, but this time without even a hint or possibility of tenderness, loud and uncompromising all the way through. The beat builds and pounds until it has reached its limits and cannot go even one measure more.

In the end
Nothin' was left
But the lies
The lies, the lies, the...

The last repetition stretches out and over what seems like an impossibly long interval.

...li-i-i-ies
We told.

On the last word of the song, the beat, having reached the edge of the chasm, dies all at once, and the sound abandons the air itself, leaving nothing but silence.

10

PETER SITS AT Ray's desk. The art has been taken down, wrapped in brown paper, and stacked against the walls. The books have been stripped from the bookshelves and packed in the cardboard boxes around the room.

It's time for group. Alex enters, highly agitated and pacing around, as if he is about to jump out of his skin, stepping and steering around the obstacle course of Ray's packed-up belongings.

"Hello, Alex," says Peter.

Distracted, Alex nods toward Peter and continues to pace.

Peter watches him. "What's going on with you, Alex?"

"I just talked to them back home. Everything's going to shit. I knew it. You know about my hit and run, right? I got a friend of mine to start checking it out. It was a young woman I hit. They took her to the hospital. That's all he's found out so far. She died! I just know she died! Or she's crippled or brain dead or…"

"You don't know any of that. Who gave you a phone pass?"

"The nurse."

Peter picks up the phone, presses a button. "Charlene, one of your nurses just gave Alex a phone pass. Since when are the nurses allowed to give phone passes?"

He listens.

"She's fired. I want her out of here right now. You take the front desk for now."

Alex, stupefied, "What kind of an asshole are you?"

Peter does not respond.

To himself more than to Peter, Alex says, "All my life, I've just wanted to help. I thought so anyway. Instead, I destroy. The nurse, the woman on the street, my family..."

"So you're responsible for the nurse?"

"Shit yes, I am! I talked her into it! She just happened to be there. In my way."

"Bullshit, Alex. You're not as powerful as you think you are. *She* made her choice. You didn't make it for her."

"I don't buy that."

"Sit down, Alex. This is the place to deal with it. And everything else."

Alex sits. Duke and Joe enter, then Maggie and Paula. All take their places and Peter joins them.

"Before we start," Peter says, "I need to share with you that I'm in a lot of pain. I need to tell you that in case it spills out in some inappropriate way. Today I told my boss to shove this job up his ass, and I think he's going to shove it up mine instead. I just fired a nurse who violated one of the most basic staff rules here. My world is chaos come. The whole community is disintegrating. And Ray. And Angel. I could have kept them apart. I knew better than to leave them together. It was their choice, but why did I have to help them make it? Plus, I gave Ray an ultimatum the other day that might just have sent him over the edge. Yeah, Alex, you're not the only one. It goes with the disease. It must be all our fault since we're the center of the world."

Alex stands. "Fuck it. Fuck this place. You can't do anything for anybody, even yourselves." Alex starts out, but before he can get out the door, Duke leaps up, rushes across the room, and tackles him. Alex struggles with Duke on the floor. "Let me go. Let me go, you asshole!"

"Fuck you, Alex," says Duke. "You ain't goin' out and dyin' on us. Not today anyway."

"Let him go, Duke," Peter says. "We can't force this on him."

Duke lets Alex up. Alex starts to leave again.

Joe screams, *"Alex! God damn it, if you can't make it, how can I?"*

"Alex," Peter barks, "would you consider listening to one thing before you go?"

Alex hesitates, turns back to look at Joe, then at Peter.

"Just listen for two minutes, that's all."

Alex, indecisive, just stands there.

"Will you sit in the circle... here with your friends?"

Alex reluctantly returns to his chair, sits down, but pulls the chair back, just outside the circle.

Peter says, "Alex, if you go, don't go for Ray or Angel. If you stay, don't stay just for Joe. If Joe can keep you here, good, but you can't do it just for him."

"We're all here for you, Alex," says Paula.

Peter says, "Do you know what your name means, Alex?"

Alex shakes his head.

"Imagine that. You go through your whole life and don't even know the meaning of your own name. I looked it up. It means 'Defender of Mankind'. Boy, that fits, doesn't it? You threw away your own cross and wanted to carry everyone else's. But that hasn't worked out so well. Because you've got to carry yours first. You've got some pain to take, some amends to make. 'Let it begin with me.' You've heard that saying, haven't you? Well, let it begin with you, Alex."

All are silent until Alex asks, "Where do you think they are now?"

"Who?"

"Ray and Angel."

"I don't care where they are. They think they're titans now. They think they can walk with the gods. We've got to stay down here on the earth. Us poor mortals, just trudging along. We're like moths to flame. Angel and Ray, their story, that's your flame. One of them anyway. Turn away. Let it go. We weren't made for flames, buddy. We were made to lie down in green pastures."

Alex shakes his head slowly back and forth. "I don't know. It's a mystery. With no solution. There was a time I thought I knew some things. And now I'm not sure I know anything. Except that I do love you people. And there are times I love the whole suffering world, every one of them, in here and out there too. And I mourn. And I grieve. For all of us. I can't help it. Ray, Angel. What does it mean?"

Peter looks around the rest of the group. "Does anyone else need to say goodbye to Ray and Angel?"

"I guess," says Maggie, "I need to say goodbye. To everyone. I've decided to leave."

Groans and small cries of concern flutter about the group.

"But I'm not going far. I'm just transferring. To a women's program."

Duke breaks the quiet this time. "Well, Maggie, I wish ya luck. Really. Nobody deserves this shit. I'm sorry. For everything."

"Despite what I said the other day, Duke, I do forgive you. Not that it's my right either to give or withhold that."

"I appreciate it, Maggie. I really do."

Maggie says, "I thought I couldn't ever cry again, but I cried in my bed last night like a little kid. For Ray and Angel if you can believe it. I wished them harm, and harm came to them. I'm not saying I caused it. But I might as well have caused it. Because I wished it. I imagined, and the world became what I imagined. 'Let it begin with me.' And, you know, I think now she never was as bad as I made her out to be. She's even a warrior in her own way."

Paula, weeping, says, "Wherever you go, remember that you helped save my life. You and Ray. Oh, Ray. I wish he could know that he saved my life…"

Peter interrupts, "Helped *you* save your life."

"But he lifted the bushel. He did. All those years, no one else ever did. No one else ever even bothered. Why wasn't that enough for him? God, Ray, walk softly."

"Are you ready to go home now?"

"I am. I'm still scared to death, but I am."

Peter turns to Joe. "Where are you, Joe?"

"Ya know, if you'd've asked me, I'd have told ya I wanted ta be just like her. I'd have told ya she had the world by the ass. And she did! God damn it, she did! But what good did it do her? No good at all. She had everything everybody in the world wants. But ya know, I'm thinkin' now, what the fuck do we want that stuff for?"

"*I*, Joe," Peter corrects him. "What do *I* want it for?"

"Yeah, what the fuck do *I* even want it for? Worship and adoration. She wanted to be worshiped, and I wanted to worship her. What in the fuck for? Her bigger than life and me smaller than life."

All are quiet until Peter says, "So who's ready to work?"

Nobody volunteers.

Peter chuckles. "Well, at least that hasn't changed. Still have to drag it out of you."

He turns, very serious now, and faces Duke. "Duke? Are you ready for what we talked about? It's gonna be hard...the hardest work of all."

Duke's eyes are closed. He nods his head.

Peter moves his chair next to Duke, takes Duke's hand. Duke's eyes remain closed.

"Okay, Duke...tell us what it's like to die."

You saw how some yearn endlessly in vain:
Such as would, else, have surely had their wish,
But have, instead, its hunger as their pain.

Dante, *Purgatorio*
(John Ciardi Translation)

ON THE LAST FRONTIER

THE EYEGLASSES JUST didn't do the trick anymore, but there was no affording new ones, so she squinted as hard as she could through the murky window smeared on the outside with grime and on the inside with the residue of accumulated cigarette smoke, whiskey breath, and half-hearted swipes of a wet but filthy rag. It looked like every one of the old gang was perched there on their respective barstools as if they had remained exactly in those places since the last time she had left them several months ago sitting on those very same stools—stools with their leather tops worn thin from broad behinds constantly sliding back and forth on them—stools subject to near-proprietary claims by those same behinds, not unlike name-plated church pews paid for with substantial and frequent cash donations from the specially favored parishioners occupying them.

Some things never changed. The poor fools still had nothing better to do on a Wednesday evening, or any evening really, than drink and jaw, and jaw, and jaw, trying in their groping, meandering, unconscious way to talk some meaning out of, or into, their lives. Good-hearted Earl with salt and pepper flat-top and the saddest eyes. Blowhard Dick, goggly eyeballs barely caged behind pop-bottle eyeglasses. Silent Sam, puffy face and slick, black hair falling almost to his shoulders. All of them about her age—except Fatuous Frank, younger than the others, with long greasy, stringy, infrequently washed hair and scraggly goatee, always seeming like the little kid tagging along after the big ones. Mel and Herb were younger too. Their stools sat empty as they had drifted to the poker machine in the corner. Jim, the bartender, lean and long but permanently stooped from bending over to talk to his customers on the bar stools, presided over the congregation with a constant wry grin and frequent mocking smile.

From the pocket of her field jacket she extracted her coin purse, one of those little rubber ones. She closed her palm and squeezed the purse on both ends to open wider a slit down the middle and counted her tiny stash, its tininess evidenced by how easily the purse opened and the amplitude of uncrowded space within. A meager bounty indeed, a lone ten-dollar bill and a few coins. After the first one or two drinks, she would have to depend on the charity of others. Disgusted, she returned the coin purse to her jacket pocket. She hesitated, trying to resist what she was certainly about to do.

Earl saw her first and waved her in, saying something to the others at the bar that she could not make out, and they too started waving her in. She continued to hold back as they kept gesticulating, getting more energetic by the second, and Earl looked like he was about to come after her. "The hell with it," she said, flung open the door, and walked in like she was a Hollywood starlet—no hesitation or indecision now, a little brash, a little arrogant, as if she had confidently made a choice.

"Katie!" the usually subdued Jim yelled, genuinely happy to see her.

"Jimmie!" she replied, returning the favor with skillfully feigned enthusiasm.

"Hey, Katie!" called Earl.

"Well, look what the wind blew down the hill!" Dick said while smacking the top of the bar with the flat of his hand.

"Where you been, Katie?" Frank asked.

Sam gestured toward a grunt that never quite came forth.

"The usual?" Jim said.

"Yes, sir." She pulled her coin purse out of her field jacket and started to finger in it for her money.

"You put that away, girl," Dick blustered.

She paid no attention, fished out the bill in the coin purse, and offered it to Jim.

"Don't take her money, Jim," Dick commanded, brandishing a small stash of bills that had been sitting on the bar in front of him, the remains of his monthly pension check.

Jim served up a shot of bourbon and two mugs of beer and set them in front of her as she kept pushing her bill at him, but he shook his head no. "Not a chance," he said. "First one's on the house."

"And the next one's on me," Dick spouted. "Where you been, girl? Haven't seen you in a coon's age."

She tossed down the shot, then took a long swallow of the beer, which nearly gagged her since she had not taken a drink for almost four months.

"Just sittin' around wastin' away, Dick. Just wastin' away."

"The hell you say," Dick said. "You don't look a inch different than you did ten years ago."

"Well, I see you haven't changed. Same old liar."

They all laughed, even Dick.

"Rainin' out there yet?" Frank asked, craning back around for a glance at the greasy front window.

"Not yet."

"It's comin' though," he said. "I can feel it. Might even be snow."

Earl slapped his palm on the bar. "Don't talk about it. It's too soon."

"Seems like it comes sooner every year," Katie said.

Frank looked mournfully into his beer mug. "The last cruise ship left tanight. Just us, now. And the snow."

"And the politicians," Dick said. "Don't forget the God-damn politicians. Tourists in the summer and politicians in the winter. Like plagues of locusts."

Katie emitted a sound of disgust. "And you'd better be thankful for 'em, Dickie. Otherwise this burg'd dry up and blow away."

"Well," Frank said, "they're already tryin' ta take the state capital away from us, ain't they? Wha'da' ya' think's gonna happen then? Just what you say, Katie. Dry up and blow away."

Dick, who was given to repeating pet gestures and phrases, again slammed his palm on the bar. "I wanna know how they can do that. Ain't it illegal or unconstitutional or somethin'? They just take a vote and rob all these people of their livelihoods. How can they do that?"

"Ask Sam," Katie said. "How do they do that, Sam?"

Sam seemed to consider whether to reply at all, then said, "Do what?"

"Rob you. Of everything you've got."

"They just do it."

"Damn right."

Dick wagged his head back and forth, trying to shake off the thought. "Now don't start that stuff, girl. The Indians are doin' just fine. The Indians are gettin' their land back. They're givin' it back to 'em. Ain't that right, Sam?"

"Didn't know that."

Katie quaffed the last of the beer in her mug. "They're 'Native Americans', Dick, not Indians. Hey, Sam, what'll ya do with it if you get it?"

"Get what?"

"The land. What'll you do with the land if they give it back to ya?"

"No idea."

"You're not gonna live on it, are ya?"

"I guess it depends where it is."

"Well, let me give ya a little tip. It isn't gonna be exactly in downtown Anchorage or anything. It's gonna be a little ways outta town, where right now there's nobody and nothin' but trees and mosquitoes and bear scat."

"Then hell no I ain't gonna live there."

"What you're gonna do is sell it. That's what you're gonna do. That's the whole point and purpose of the thing. You're gonna sell it and take the money they give ya and buy a snowmobile and enough whiskey ta last ya for a few months." She glanced back and forth, addressing the group. "Then at the end of the year he's out of money. And who's got the land? The white man, that's who. It's just a big land grab, that's all it is. They'll take it from the taxpayers, launder it through the Natives—sorry about that, Sam, just another screwin'—and eventually build it up in condos and parkin' garages and shoppin' centers and convenience stores."

Frank was so agitated he stood up to proclaim, "And I say good for 'em. Put that land ta productive use."

"What productive use is that?" Katie said.

"Goods and services, that's what."

"You ain't got enough? Want another place ta buy more of the same junk you've already got? Is that what ya want?"

Dick waved his empty mug at Jim to order another. "You talk like a damn Communist or somethin'. You better watch out. Ronnie Reagan's gonna do the Commies in, sure as hell, just like he did the damn unions, and you'll all be S-O-L."

"And he'll probably get us all blown to smithereens while he's at it. What for? That's all I'm saying. What for?"

She finished the second beer. "Jimmy, please, another. You still buyin', Dick, even for a Communist?"

"I gave my word, didn't I?"

Earl cocked his head back as if he had given the issue considerable thought and said, "I think Katie's right. It's like the parkin' garage down by the wharf. Big, ugly thing. It'll make the whole town ugly. But they just shove it down our throats. They took the land...

"Wha' da ya mean?" Frank interrupted. "The downtown merchants need that garage ta survive. Don't they, Jimmie?"

Jim shrugged an "I don't know" and said, "I ain't no merchant. I just work here."

"Well, they do. They need it."

"What for?" Katie said again and chugged the shot of bourbon Jimmie had just set down in front of her. "So they can fleece the tourists some more?"

"Well, Madam Mao," said Frank, proud of himself for conceiving that reference, "ain't that what the tourists come up here for in the first place?"

They all flinched at a sudden commotion in the corner. A dispute had erupted, and Mel had slammed Herb into the poker machine. Herb leaped back at him. Punching wild roundhouses at each other with zero percent accuracy, then staggering around clumsily wrestling each other, knocking over chairs and bumping against tables, they finally ended up grappling on the floor, rolling over and over again.

Jim rushed from behind the bar to separate them. Dick, gleeful, eyes bulging with excitement, slid off his stool, crouched like a wrestling referee in a ring, and cried, "Let 'em go, Jimmie. They can't hurt nothin' but themselves. Let 'em go."

"Jackasses," Earl said.

"Need some help, Jimmie?" said Dick, not about to help.

Sam and Earl joined Jim to separate the brawlers. Flanked on either side by Earl and Sam, Jim pushed both the combatants toward the door. "Now get on outta' here before I decide to kick *both* your behinds."

Jim, Sam, and Earl returned to the bar while Dick waddled over to the window to observe. After a short interval, he turned and reported, "Fight's over. They're just cussin' each other now."

"One's scared and the other's glad of it," Katie said. She felt herself getting drunk. Too quickly. Couldn't hold it like she used to. Been off the sauce too long.

"Yep, there's the proof," said Frank. "Winter's comin' alright. Everybody starts goin' crazy one at a time. Pretty soon the shotguns'll start goin' off all over the hills up there."

"Yep," said Dick, still watching out the window, his back to the bar. "Believe it or not, they're goin' on down Franklin Street like nothin' unfriendly ever happened."

He ambled back from the window and stood next to Katie, put his arm around her and pulled her toward him until their faces almost touched, and would have touched if she hadn't stiffened up. "God, Katie, it reminds me of the old days. You remember? Me and George would stand toe to toe and whip them all. Remember that?"

She pushed herself away from him so hard she almost fell backward off her stool. "Not exactly."

Dick, undaunted and missing the signal, as drunks do, said, "Good ol' times. You heard from ol' George lately?"

"Some."

"How's he doin'? Not frozen ta death yet?"

"Says he's doin' fine."

Dick wiggled back up on his stool. "Well, he's survived two winters up there on the last frontier, and you didn't think he'd make one. Crazy as he is, ya gotta admire the man for his spunk. That took guts at his age. The pioneer spirit. Ol' George had it after all, he sure did." He paused for effect, then, with a leer, added, "He got him a new girlfriend up there yet?"

"Guess not. The fool keeps wanting me ta come up there with him."

Dick guffawed, nearly shouting, "Well, maybe that's where you belong, girl. No parkin' garages or convenience stores up there on the Yukon!"

Frank, leering too, chimed in, "Yeah. Ya don't like progress, ya oughtta go on up there and live easy off the land."

"Progress, my foot. The only thing we're progressin' to is the grave. *That's* the last frontier, Dick."

"Don't start that doomsday stuff on me now, you old gloomy Gus."

"Think about it, boys. Death. That's what it's all about, isn't it? That's why they're building all that stuff out there, isn't it? If they keep rootin' and scrapin' and developin' and tearin' up the earth, then they don't have ta think about dyin', at least for a while."

"That's nonsense," Frank said. "What about jobs?"

"What about jobs?" She held up her mug to Jim. "Another, Jimmy, please. Just the beer this time."

"You want everybody ta lose their jobs...have another Great Depression?"

"I already live in the Great Depression, Frankie boy," Katie said.

Frank, increasingly drunkenly belligerent, said, "If your job disappeared, you sure wouldn't like it."

"When's the last time *you* had a job, Frankie?"

"That's my choice. I could get a job anytime I want."

"Doing what?"

"Anything I put my mind to. It's a free country, ain't it?"

"But some's freer than others, aren't they now?"

"You old people are enough ta depress a young man ta death, ya know that?"

"Say, Katie," Earl said, "speakin' a jobs, don't you work the night shift? You're here a little early, aren't ya? You get off early tonight?"

She grimaced. "Yeah, real early. And real permanently."

"They laid ya off?"

"Well, you could call it that, I guess."

"You quit?"

"Not exactly."

"Come on. What happened?"

"They fired me."

"They didn't! How could they?"

"Well, I've got to admit I didn't give 'em a whole lot of choice."

Dick's right eyebrow cocked up. "What happened?" he said suspiciously.

"Some big shot came in. One of those guys that come up here ta fish in a thousand dollars' worth of clothes from L.L. Bean. One of those guys that just reels 'em in by the hundred and throws 'em back in again. And he was drunk and mean as hell, and the Bloody Marys weren't spicy enough, and the soup was cold, and the steak was like an old shoe heel, and I ran back and forth and kept kissin' his fanny, but he kept on abusin' me like it was my fault that the bartender's drunker than the customers, and the cook's a dunce, and the hotel's just one big overpriced dump. And when he wasn't abusin' me, he was braggin' about all the fish he'd caught and all the bears he'd killed. And, finally, he just exasperated me, and so I said, 'Young man, I may be your waitress, but I'm not your slave.'"

"Good for you," Early spluttered.

"So he calls the manager over and says, real loud too, 'I want another waitress. Put this old broad in a nursing home and get me someone that was born in the 20th century.'"

Dick and Frank laughed but quickly stifled themselves, looking guilty and sheepish.

"So I squinted at him and said, 'I hope one of those bears you hunt down chews you up and spits you out like the little puddle of puke you are.'"

Outraged, Earl could hardly control himself. "And they fired ya for *that*?"

"Oh, Katie," Dick said, "that vicious tongue of yours. Mark my words, it'll be the demise of you yet."

"No, Earl," she said, "they didn't fire me for that. They fired me when I dumped the little pipsqueak's plate right in his lap."

"My lord, Katie!" Frank cried out.

Dick shook his head in disapproval. "When're you gonna grow up?"

Earl shook his head in disbelief. "So they fired ya? For *that*?" he repeated.

"On the spot. Wouldn't even give me my paycheck or the tip money from the credit cards."

Earl, all solidarity, said, "Give this lady another one on me, Jim."

"Well," said Dick, "wha'da'ya expect, Earl? She put 'em in a hell of a pickle. I'll bet he's callin' his lawyer right now."

"He was a lawyer himself," Katie said.

Jim laughed. Frank brought both hands to his face and groaned.

"He'll sue for a million dollars, mark my words," Dick said.

"Well, he can have all I've got, which is exactly nothin'."

"No, Katie," said Frank. "The hotel. He'll sue the hotel."

Katie quickly downed the shot Jim had just served her. "Well," she said, "if that's what this country's come to, so be it. There was a time when no jury'd give that man a dime. Add a beer to that, Jimmie, will ya? That shot didn't go down so easy."

"Christ, Katie, what'll you do now?" said Jim as he drew her another beer from the tap. She shrugged and stared down at the cigarette burns in the wood of the bar. "Need a barmaid around here?"

"It's almost winter," Jim said sadly. "The tourists are gone."

Dick said, more maliciously than solicitously, "When this gets out, nobody'll hire ya."

"What're you gonna do?" Frank said. "How'll you eat?"

"Well, that's probably the one thing I've got goin' in my direction right now. I've got fish laid up."

"How much?" Dick asked in a prosecutorial tone.

"A bunch. Maybe seventy pounds so far."

Dick continued his interrogation, raising the belligerent tone a notch. "Where in the world did you get seventy pounds of fish?"

"I caught 'em."

Dick made a scoffing sound in his throat. "I remember a time when you wouldn't get within four feet of a fish. For eatin' anyway."

"And there was a time when I wasn't old and beat and hungry."

"And how'd ya learn ta fish? You used ta not know one end of a rod from the other."

"Jesus, Dick," she said, growing more uncomfortable and evasive as the interrogation proceeded, "you're the nosiest old man on the face of the earth."

"Come on. How'd ya learn?"

"Well, if you must know, Reuben taught me."

"Reuben? You gotta be shittin'. Now that calls for another round. All around, Jim," Dick cried out, waving his hand back and forth, indicating drinks for everyone at the bar.

"The 'Reuben' that used ta drink in here?" Jim asked.

"The one and only," said Katie.

"Thank ya, Dick," Frank said, then to Katie, "The stargazer? The little guy carries the little telescope hangin' from his belt loop, crazier'n a loon?"

"I didn't think he could tie his own shoes," Earl said.

"I thought he was dead," Jim said sadly.

"He isn't dead, and he isn't an idiot either. He's just a might wet-brained, that's all. He's just got a touch of Korsakoff's or somethin'."

"Korsakoff's!" Dick exclaimed. "Now that's a damn big word for ya. What in the world is that?"

"What you've had all your life. Wet brain. From drinkin' too much Sterno and Aqua Velva."

Dick grimaced in disgust. "Boy, you're keepin' some fine company these days, aren't ya? Bein' taken care of by a idiot!"

"Which is a darn sight better than nothin'. What's anybody else gonna do for me?"

"Maybe you just need ta ask."

"Ask who? You? What would you ever give me except thirty seconds in the evening and a pair of dirty drawers in the morning?"

Everyone but Dick laughed at that, even Sam.

Dick said, "I bought you a drink, didn't I? Right here tonight, didn't I? Two of 'em even."

"You did, I'll give you that."

"And what thanks do I get? Your vicious tongue, that's what I get."

"If I gave you anything else, you wouldn't know what to do with it."

They laughed even harder this time, Dick again excepted, who, instead snorted a sneer out his nose. "What do you and the idiot do? Guzzle the liquor and sit around and babble at each other?"

"He doesn't drink anymore."

"Impossible," Frank pronounced.

"I don't believe it," Dick said.

"Like anyone cares what you believe. But whether you believe it or not, it's true all the same."

Dick, ratcheting the belligerence up a notch, said, "How're you gonna pay your rent? Your heat bill?"

"Well, I've got my Social Security."

"Social Security! You can't keep a dog on that."

"Well, this old dog'll just hafta keep somehow."

"But honest, Katie," Earl said, "what'll you do now?"

She gave that a little thought. "Maybe it's time ta take that walk in the woods. Just walk 'til I drop. Freeze ta death in the snow. They won't find me 'til spring. Or maybe I'll just stick my head in my old gas oven."

"Don't be morbid, woman," Dick said.

"Well, that's exactly what I'm gonna do when it's time."

"What time?" said Frank.

"When I can't help myself anymore."

"Hell, you can't help yourself now," said Dick. "Dependin' on a idiot."

"So be it. Maybe it's time then. At least I won't hafta listen to you anymore."

"That's it. Run me off. Just like ya run everybody else off all your life. Either ya run them off or you run off from them."

"Dick!" Jim warned.

Katie flinched and searched for her chest with her chin. Frank looked away. Even Sam reacted, squirming a little. They all knew what Dick meant.

Earl rose from his stool, swayed a bit back and forth, and said, "Now that's about a God-damn 'nough, Dick."

"Well, think about it," Dick said. "She had a fine husband, didn't she? Until she run ol' George off too."

"I said that was enough!" Earl said, advancing on Dick.

Katie threw up her arm, stopping Earl's advance. "Leave him alone. I don't pay any attention to the damn fool anyway."

Dick would not be put off. "That's what ya need ta do. Mark my words. Ya need ta go on up there to the Yukon with George."

"The hell with George."

"Pride! That's it, ain't it? Well, Pride goes before the downfall."

She paused again, thinking about it, then said, not mawkishly but as a simple fact, "Be pretty hard for me to fall any farther, Dick. Pretty hard. I've reached the bottom, I think."

"God," said Frank, "you old people are depressin'. Can I have another, Jimmie?"

A sudden silence prevailed for a time. Unable to bear it any longer, Frank went on, "Anybody go to the party tonight?"

"What party?" Earl said.

"You live on another planet or what? The Love Boat party. The farewell party. Its last trip up this way. They had a party for it. Speeches and toasts. Some of 'em was even cryin'. It'll go down in history. September 12, 1984."

"You'd cry too," Earl said, "if your golden goose was just floatin' on away."

"Love Boat, my foot," Katie said, "Death Boat is more like it."

"There you go again," Dick said. "What's that supposed ta mean?"

"Have you ever bothered to get your chin outta your beer long enough ta look up and see who comes off those cruise ships and ferry boats? Huh? You ever? Old people, that's who. I must've served ten thousand of 'em up at the hotel. And ya know what they say, darn near every one of 'em? 'We just had ta come up here and see all this before we die.' They call that waterway out there the Marine Highway, but they ought-ta call it the Highway of Death. That's why I won't go up ta George. I'll starve. I'll freeze ta death before I set foot on one of those damn boats. Just like walkin' right into the grave."

"You're crazy, ya know that?" Dick scoffed. "You gettin' senile or what?"

"Maybe I am, but I'm not gettin' on that boat."

"Well," said Frank, "there ain't no other way out of here except by plane, so I reckon you're stuck."

"I'll bring flowers to your funeral, girl," Dick said.

Earl, wavering tipsily on his stool, said, "We all have ta go sometime, Katie."

"Well, I'm not quite ready yet if it's all the same ta you. It scares me stiff. You ever thought about it? *Really* thought about it? *Blink.* Lights off. Forever. The end."

"Now what're ya sayin'," Dick said, "now ya tellin' us ya don't be-lieve in God?"

"No, I don't. Or heaven either."

Dick waved his hand at her in dismissal. "Well, no wonder. No won-der you're such a sorry case. Ya don't have no reason ta live then. Ya might as well take your walk in the woods."

"You think you're goin' to heaven, do you? You really think you're gonna live forever?"

"If I'm a good man, I sure will."

"You can forget that then," Jim said.

That one brought a smile from Sam and belly laughs from all the rest, and even Dick chuckled a little.

"Let's suppose there was a God like you say," Katie said. "He'd have some things to answer for in my book, but let's just suppose he's a pretty good fella after all. Where does heaven follow from that? Don't animals die? Don't stars die? Don't whole galaxies explode out there in the universe every single day? Why should we humans be different than everything else in God's world?"

"'Cause it wouldn't have no purpose then, that's why."

"So you think it's all got a purpose? Let me ask ya this then. What's the purpose of that fella up north that chopped up his wife with a cleaver—while she was alive! What might be the purpose of that? And you know what he said when she screamed 'Oh God help me!'? He said, 'Shut up, bitch. If there was a God, this wouldn't be happenin' to you.' He confessed to the police that he said that."

"I don't believe it."

"It was in the paper a couple days ago."

"That's just plain evil."

"They oughtta do the same exact thing ta him as he did ta her," Frank said.

"Who made this world, Dick?" Katie said.

"God of course. God made this world."

"Who made evil then?"

"Not God. It's just a trial. A test."

"Kinda like a big cosmic game show, huh?"

"Stop it! Stop it right now." He looked up fearfully. "You're lucky God doesn't strike you down!"

Katie looked up, offering herself to heaven. "Come on! Strike me down!"

"Now you're a blasphemer!"

Dick laboriously and very carefully raised himself off his stool, took a step toward Katie, swayed back and forth, and said, "I've had enough from you. Jim, it's her or me."

"Come on, Dick," Jim said.

"I won't be put off, Jim. I'm too good a customer ta have ta endure this woman's insults. Either she goes or I go."

"Come on, Dick."

"So you think I'm bluffin', do ya?"

He tried to stomp, but mostly just staggered, to the door.

"Come on, Dick," Jim pleaded to Dick's departing back.

Dick passed through the door, then stuck his head back in and yelled at Katie, "You're gettin' exactly what you deserve, woman. Exactly what you deserve."

"Should I go after him?" Frank asked.

"Screw him," Earl said.

"He'll be back," Jim said.

"I'm sorry, Jimmie," Katie said. "But he's a pompous fool."

"Such a damn know-it-all," Earl muttered.

"He don't mean no harm," Frank said.

Earl looked at Dick's empty stool. "Hell, he don't mean nothin' at all."

They didn't have much to say after that. Dick's departure seemed to take the edge off Katie and off the evening itself. Before long, Sam slid off his stool without a word and went to play the poker machine, and the rest of them lapsed into desultory and increasingly incoherent talk as the bar slowly emptied toward closing time. When Katie realized she could not finish the beer in front of her, she laid her left arm flat on the bar, crossed her right arm over it, rested her head down on both, and fell quickly asleep. At closing time she remained there, passed out in the same position.

"Guess she can't hold it so much anymore," Earl said. "Good ol' girl though, believe that."

"She surely is that," Jim said. "I'll call a cab."

"I'll ride with her," Earl said, "and make sure she gets in her front door okay."

Earl reached over and patted her gently on the back as Jim made the phone call.

Frank shook his head. "Old people," he said. "Depressin'."

"You'll be there yourself before you know it," Jim said. "Want another for the road?"

"No thanks, Jimmie, full up here. In fact, got to go piss some of it out."

On his way to the toilet Frank stopped and looked out the window, made a noise of astonishment, turned around, and said, "I'll be God-damned if I don't think it might snow tonight."

Jim shook his head.

"No way," Earl said.

Frank looked back outside again. "Seems like it comes earlier every year."

KATIE LIVED IN a small apartment carved out of the first floor of a house that had once been painted in bright yellow with light blue trim but had faded and peeled to a dessicated husk of its former vibrant self. Earl had managed to help Katie into the apartment and deposit her on the couch in her living room where she now sprawled fully-clothed in whiskey-sodden sleep. During the night and the mercifully sunless drizzly Juneau morning, she had occasionally stirred toward consciousness, but like a fox from hounds, her mind raced away from the unwelcome invading memories chasing her from the day and night before. But now she vaguely sensed irritating, continuous, and progressively amplified noises that even boozy sleep could not entirely resist. These originated from outside the house, on the front porch, where a small balding man wearing the Juneau uniform of rubber rain slicker and rubber boots that rose to just below his knees, clutched two fishing rods in one hand and pounded frantically on the front door with the other, yelling things like "Hey!" and "Katie, you in there?"

He paused for a moment and pressed his ear against the door. Hearing nothing, whimpering a little, he dropped the fishing rods, scurried over to a small window and looked in. Frustrated, he rushed back to the door, rapidly turned the knob, cried out wordlessly in panic when it didn't give, and began throwing his body against the door, trying to break it open. The weak old damp wood gave way quickly, the jamb split, and he burst inside.

Seeing Katie on the couch, not a flicker of movement from her, he said, "Uh-oh," and went to her. He stood over her, reached down, and began to shake her.

"You dead? You dead now already?"

Now fully awake but not immediately realizing where she might be, her eyes popping in terror, she groaned loudly and rose up abruptly. A sinew seemed to snap in her neck. She jumped up from the couch, and rushed into the kitchen. He remained standing by the couch, listening to her gagging and, ultimately, vomiting. After a few moments of silence, she came and stood in the opening from the kitchen to the living room, grabbing the door jamb to steady herself.

"Reuben, what the hell!" she said.

"I thought you was dead," he whined.

"You nearly killed me alright."

"You been drinkin'," he said accusingly. "You been drinkin' again."

"How'd you get in here?"

He pointed at the front door. Her uncertain footsteps followed the direction of his finger to the door, which he had failed to close. She surveyed the heavily splintered jamb and tried to shut the door, which now wouldn't close all the way.

"Look what you did!"

"You been drinkin'."

She closed the door and continued to survey the damage. "How'm I gonna fix this?"

"Time ta go fishin'," he said as if this were a perfectly natural response to her question.

"No fishin' taday."

"Got to. Be winter soon. No fishin' then."

"*Not* today," she said with threatening emphasis.

She sat down on the couch, and he sat in an overstuffed chair across from her. For a while neither of them said anything. He just stared at the floor, lost in wherever it was that his mind took him at these times.

Finally, she said, "What're you doin' over there?"

He looked up at her. "You been drinkin'. I know it."

"Yeah, I have. So what?"

"You gonna die. Deader than a donut."

"Doornail."

"What door?"

"It's not a donut. It's 'deader than a doornail.' That's the saying."

"The door ain't dead. You're gonna be dead."

"You can bet on that for sure."

"You're gonna be a sad cadaver."

"And that's also the truth."

"Maybe sometime you oughtta say a prayer, old woman."

"And what would I pray for?"

He looked confused for a moment, then burst out, "Thank you, God-damn it. That's what you say."

"Thank who for what?"

"The couch there," pointing to it, and, pointing upward, "the roof above and the sky above that, the God-damn fishes in the sea, the hair on your old head, the moon…"

"Alright, Reuben, I get it."

"…the trees, the snow on the ground, the bats and the bulls, the mice and the crows…"

"Okay!"

…dogs and cats, brains and bathrooms, clocks, and cars and crooked stiles…" His litany had become self-perpetuating.

"Stop it, Reuben!"

"…donuts, doornails, and dog shit; prunes and peas and puffin birds…"

"Stop!"

135

"...otters and ocean waves, wild cats and wild blueberries..."

She screamed this time. "*Stop!*"

He pointed an accusing finger at her. "Surrender. You better surrender. Or I won't hope for you no more at all."

"I thought you wanted some coffee."

"No. *You* want coffee. *I* ain't been drinkin'. *You* been drinkin'."

"Do you want some coffee or not?"

"You got coffee?"

"Just enough for a last pot. It's loaded up and ready to go. Just light the burner and put it on."

"That's the best idea you had all day." He jumped up and scooted to the kitchen.

She yelled after him, "Be careful of the gas. Don't blow your fool self up."

The kitchen was quiet for a long time. Too quiet too long. Just as she was about to force herself up to check on him, he returned with a mug of coffee in each hand. He had filled the mugs to their brims, and some of the coffee splashed out onto the floor as he bounded toward her.

"Hold 'er there, Knute," she said, raising her hands in warning, trying to slow him down, which succeeded just in time. She carefully put both hands on the cup and took it from him. He plopped on the couch next to her, spilling some of the coffee on his pants.

"Who's Knute?" he said.

"Nobody you know."

"It's cold in here."

"And gonna get colder."

"What time is it?"

"Three o'clock."

"You better get to work."

"No work today."

"Is it Sunday already?"

"Thursday."

"That's a workday."

"No work anymore."

"You retired, huh?" He laughed loud and slapped his hand on the couch.

"They fired me," she said, almost in tears.

"You was drunk, wasn't you?" he said mournfully.

"No, I wasn't drunk."

He wagged his head back and forth in a "no, no, no" gesture, and little tears squeezed out of his eyes. "Never gonna learn. Never, never. Drunk and got fired."

"I *told* you I wasn't drunk!"

But he was inconsolable. "Drunk and got fired. Happens every time. Down, down, down."

"I said—" But she decided in mid-sentence that it was hopeless.

He dug his hand in his pocket and pulled out a few soiled bills and thrust them at her. "You need money. I got money for you."

"Put your money away."

He threw the bills in her lap.

"I never met a more stubborn fool in my life."

He turned his head away from her and looked straight ahead, and she had known him long enough that she knew exactly what was happening. He had snapped abruptly away from her, had stumbled into some obscure crevice of his brain that had captured him and held him fast and would do so for an indeterminate amount of time.

She watched him for a while, then called to him. "Reuben." He failed to respond, so she said louder, "Reuben!"

He twitched and looked at her, seeming not to know where he was.

"Ya know, you're just drivin' over on the access lane while the rest of us are drivin' down the freeway."

"I don't drive no more."

He drifted away again. Sometimes he would stay that way for many minutes, even hours. She wondered what journey of the mind he might have embarked on now. She actually envied him—a brain-damaged man, yes, but a man mercifully unburdened by too many memories. She, on the other hand, had far too many memories, almost all of them painful. Watching Reuben sitting in that chair reminded her of Clyde, who used to sit and sit the same way, and that took her back to the beginning, her Genesis so to speak, or, more accurately, her Fall from the Garden, so long ago, in 1953, when she was only twenty-eight years old and lived in Kansas City with Clyde and the two kids—Randall born when she was only nineteen, and Marcy right after, when she was only twenty. So damn stuck. Clyde wasn't the worst fellow in the world by any means. He had a good job at the GM plant down in Leeds, didn't drink too awful much, didn't beat her. But no affection. Just sitting in his chair, night after night, reading the paper and listening to the radio, the damn baseball games every night in the summer, the announcers droning on. Not wanting to talk at all. Or do much else either. They would have sex hardly ever, and even then pretty much only when he was liquored up, the old "slam bam, thank ya, ma'am." Actually, there was no "thank ya" involved. He would just turn over, show her his back, and push his snore button while she would lie there wishing for more, believing there just had to be more. The one time she tried to start up something with him when they were both cold sober, he had acted like she was some kind of Jezebel.

People had always said how pretty she was and how fine her figure was, and *she* still was and *it* still was despite her having given birth twice. But it was all wasted on Clyde. And, to top everything off, he had announced his plan to move his nasty old mother in without even consulting Katie—his wife after all, a humble handmaiden maybe, but not a slave with no rights at all. Yet she had to be careful with that line of thinking--danger of excuses and rationalizations. It was the being stuck that must have gotten to her, made her so vulnerable, knowing that the rest of her life was going to be *that,* just *that* and nothing more. Forever. Or at least her little piece of forever.

And then George returned home from his stint in the army during the Korean War, full of big dreams about migrating back to Alaska where he'd been stationed. The three of them had been friends since high school. Indeed she and George had dated once upon a time. But her parents hadn't cared much for him. She guessed they could tell right off that he was more of a talker and a dreamer than a dependable working family man type like Clyde. So they'd discouraged the teenagers in every way they could. Parents were so full of power in those days. And despite all the years away from each other, and all that had happened to her in those intervening years, she having married and borne two children and all, George still harbored a crush on her. He kept hanging around, buddying up with Clyde, but she suspected both his motives and his methods right from the start.

For a long time she kept clear of him. But one night, as she watched over a pot roast in the kitchen while George and Clyde sat on the front porch drinking beer, George sauntered into the kitchen with two empty beer bottles and looking sneaky.

"More beer already? You boys better slow down."

"Come on out and join us."

"What for? Clyde doesn't want me out there."

"Well, I want you out there, and I'm the guest."

"Seems like you're getting to be more house mate than house guest."

"You know, you're still such a looker," he said and sidled up next to her. He put his arm around her and tried to kiss her.

She pushed him away. "What're you doin'? You better watch yourself."

But he just winked at her, not chagrined in the slightest. "I'd rather watch *you.*"

She pushed him again. "Get out!"

But she wasn't as angry as those words implied, and that was the fateful moment, the turning point as she later came to see it. She wasn't really angry. Much as she'd tried to resist it, she was excited, a slight but distinct pounding in her chest and a pleasurable stirring somewhere else.

After dinner, they sat on the porch drinking beer, George going on and on about Alaska. "No place like it in the world, I'll tell ya that. You two've got to come up there with me. Can you take a vacation this summer, Clyde? We'll hop the train to Seattle, and we can catch a boat up the Inside Passage ta Juneau. The damn beauty of that boat ride is just sinful."

Clyde shook his head in a scoffing manner. "If I do take a vacation, it won't be to go up and stare at trees and ice and Eskimos, that's for sure."

"You don't know what you're sayin'. The world's brand new up there. I mean it literally. There's places all over where the ice is still recedin' and the land just emergin'. Just rocks at first, then a little moss maybe, then a little damn bug or two, and then the birds come ta eat the bugs, then sediment builds, the earth just builds itself. And then there's grass, and then trees, and pretty soon a forest. Then the bigger animals come. Life emergin', Clyde. A new world. Green. Green as heaven. Misty as heaven too. And silent. Like you're alone with God at the edge of the world."

"Well, I don't know as He and I'd have much to talk about. I bet they don't even have movies up there yet."

"They hardly have anything at all up there yet. And that's the beauty of it. It's the last frontier. Nothin' but opportunity. I'm goin'. I tell ya I'm goin' for good."

"Eskimo George."

"If ya wanted to, you could live right off the land. Grow a garden in the summer, put away some of the fruit and vegetables for the winter, and hunt and trap and fish for your protein. But there's towns too. And they need everything, Clyde."

"That's fine talk for a bachelor like you. But I got a family ta support. Right, Katie?"

Since he really expected no response, she did not give one.

"And," George said, "you'll keep workin' the night shift 'til ya drop on the sidewalk on the way home from work one mornin'. And what'll it have all been for, Clyde?"

"At least I'll have done my duty."

"Ah, crap. Duty-schmooty. What about you, Katie?"

"Well, George, maybe it's just dreams, but I guess dreams are worth havin'."

Clyde waved her right off. "Dreams, my eye. Jawin'. That's all it is. Jawin'. Get me another beer. Want another, George?"

She did not put much stock in what George said about Alaska being the whole world starting over, but she had to think kindly of a man that had such powerful dreams and was apparently willing to travel to the very end of the earth to pursue them. Especially when she was so *stuck* herself. Looking back on it time after time, too many times, over the years, more than once she had wondered if she might have had such dreams herself, stuffed and stifled and buried so far down that they never even managed to struggle to the surface for even a moment. Which might have made her resistance very low one night when George sneaked over to the house when Clyde was at work, and they both got a little drunk, and sly George knew exactly what to do then.

Naked under his nakedness, she smiled up at him and said, "You devil, you got your way after all."

"And you loved every minute of it."

"I did."

And then something happened to her that never had before. He gave her a long, slow, gentle kiss.

"I'll be back tomorrow," he said.

She pushed him off and sat up. "No. This is it. There's kids in this house. And a husband."

"You're goin' to Alaska with me. That's what you're gonna do."

"I've got *kids*, George."

"Yeah, you've got kids. And when they're off on their own in ten years, what'll ya have then? A mean, nasty old husband with a mean, nasty old mother in your house. And they'll make a mean, nasty old woman out of you too. At only thirty-eight years old. Just an old woman goin' ta funerals. That's all they talk about around here. That's all they *do* around here is go ta funerals!" And, puffed up and proud at having delivered such a rousing exit speech, he marched out of her house.

Of course he did come back. She sometimes wondered what would have happened, or, more importantly, *not* happened, if Clyde hadn't worked the night shift. She and George carried on a regular intrigue—lots of sneaking around, smuggling George in and out of the house after dark, making him park his car blocks away and walk to her house, living in constant fear that one of the kids would wake up and walk in on them, or that Clyde would take sick and come home from work early without calling, or that they would doze off and sleep through the night to wake to quite a surprise in the morning. Or that, despite all their precautions, someone would still witness something and tongues would start to wag, or who knows how many other unfortunate possibilities.

But she just couldn't give it up. And George got it in his head how wonderful it would be if they could spend some truly private time making love in a motel room. Where they could have no care about an intrusion—where they could talk as loud as they wanted, cry out in the ecstasy they were forced to stifle there in her house where they were constantly shushing each other—a truly private place where they could freely roam around in, and on, and over, and up and down, each other's bodies in every way they couldn't let themselves be free to do in her house.

So they concocted a story to tell Clyde about George volunteering to take her to some sappy romantic movie that Clyde would never go see, and George was gracious enough not only to waste his time accompanying her but would himself pay for the babysitter. Why Clyde ever swallowed that one she'd never know, but he did, oblivious to the end. But deep down, in addition to all the other things they sought from a night alone together in a motel room, they must also have wanted very badly to fall gently asleep in each other's arms, in a bed instead of on a couch or the floor, because that's what they ended up doing. And she didn't wake up until a streak of daylight stabbed through a gap in the window curtain and right into her mind and then her heart. When she called Clyde, he didn't give her a chance to say a word, he just said, "You whore, I never want to see your face again, and you can forget about ever seein' your children again either."

He hung up, and, just like that, her old life ended.

George said he would go and demand that Clyde give up her clothes, but she could not bear, on top of what she had already done, to provoke such a scene. She could not even face her own parents, who, she knew, would side with Clyde. And that was exactly what they did as soon as they got the chance. It was 1953. She had stayed out all night copulating with a man not her husband. Women just did not do such things back then. "Not "respectable" women anyway. Never. At least never in a place like Kansas City—not and got away with it anyway.

She considered waiting it out so that someday she might be able to see her children again, but they would surely be taught to hate her and be mortified in every cell of their bodies that they had been cursed to be born of such a mother. So it was either stay there with that word "Whore" branded on her or give in to George and his great Alaska adventure. It didn't take too many drinks, plus a seemingly infinite despair, to convince her to take off with him across the flatlands, leaving Kansas City and every bit of her old life irretrievably behind, except for George and a burden of guilt and shame that would torment her the rest of her years. She often asked herself why hadn't just jumped out of that speeding car and ended it right there. Cowardice, that's why.

Somewhere in Kansas they stopped in a diner and had what they call a "Come to Jesus." Up to that point they had been so quiet, hardly said a word—even George, which must have been very hard on such a gabber as him. But she could tell he was building up to something. Before their food came, food she had no hope of actually eating, he set his coffee cup down with a firm little thud, prelude to an announcement. "You might not believe me, but I am as sorry as I can be that I brought this on. But I don't know what to do about it now. I'm thinkin' that some part of you must hate me right now. And I'll do anything you say ta try and make it up to ya."

"That's not it. I don't blame *you*. I just want to die of shame."

"If you can make sense of it, we'll turn around and go back."

"That's the problem. I can't make sense of it. Doesn't seem like anything to do but go on."

"Do we have any chance of bein' happy?"

"This may not be the right time to try to answer that. All I can think of right now is there are two children back there need a mother."

"And there's a woman and a man right here that need a life, fools or worse that they may be."

"Just seems like I don't deserve anything good anymore."

"You know, we were raised to believe that there's no sin that can't be forgiven."

"Maybe. But that's only after you pay the right penance."

"Seems to me you've already paid it, and more than enough."

"That's too easy, George. Seems to me you always want to take the easy way out."

"Well, I wonder how much of this 'shame,' as you're callin' it, is really about those kids, or is it really just about what the adults are thinkin' and sayin' about you back there. If it's just all selfish, then it probably isn't really penance, is it?"

She bristled at that, though she knew it was close to the truth. George should have just left her there by the side of the road and gone on with his life, which now, with her, would never be even close to what he'd dreamed it could be.

"I love you, Katie. Nobody in this world loves you like I do. Certainly not that damn fool Clyde. Not even your kids. They didn't choose you. But I did. I *chose* you. All those years after your parents did us in, I kept that flame goin'. It's still burnin' bright too, now more than ever." She wanted to tell him his damn flame had burnt them both to cinders. But she held back. All they had left was each other, and what they had wasn't all bad. That night in the motel, she wrote Clyde a letter, telling him she was so sorry, and that, if he could find it in his soul to do so, please tell the children she loved them and that if she could ever do anything to help make it up to him or to them, she would do it, no quibbles or even questions. She worried that the children would never see the letter, that Clyde would just throw it in the trash, so she wrote out a second copy and sent it to her mother, who might someday have the chance and be willing to show it to the kids. And George and Katie managed to make love that night, for the first time since that fateful other night in that motel room back in Kansas City, and it was so good she still remembered it.

During all of that trip across the country she kept trying to make the best of an impossible situation, and it was certainly an adventure for a girl who had never, not once, been out of Kansas City. Her only summer vacations with her family, and then with Clyde, had consisted of a week in a tiny rented cabin on a tacky little lake in a scruffy little town just outside of Kansas City. And here they were, sinners that they were, traveling through paradise after paradise—through Santa Fe and Albuquerque and on into eastern Arizona through the world of the Navajos, then on to Flagstaff sitting there at the foot of the San Francisco Peaks, sacred mountains according to the Indians out there, the center of the world. And they saw the Grand Canyon too, and from there moved on up to the stunning red-rock fantasia of Utah. In Idaho somewhere they picked up the Lewis and Clark Trail. Then Montana.

God, Montana! There were a hundred places along the way she'd just as soon've stopped at and stayed forever. Empty, silent spaces. Room for the soul—even hers, in such bad shape as it surely was. But it was Alaska they were heading for, the last frontier. Cruising down the highway beside the Columbia River in Oregon, just like Lewis & Clark, her soul seemed to soar and she felt exalted despite everything.

In Seattle they boarded the boat to Alaska, and it was just in time because they had only a little money left. The Inside Passage was just as beautiful as George had described. It seemed like a virgin world, pure and impossible to violate, and that realization caused her heart to break yet again. Then Juneau—journey's end, it turned out—but it seemed like a paradise too. What reason was there to go on to anywhere else? Whales and fish just jumping out of the water all over Auke Bay. Pretty little pastel-painted houses dotting the foothills. The mountain towering over the town nestled beneath it, like a big brother dedicated to protecting its younger one from harm.

Good people too for the most part. Not that she and George were any great addition. George got a crappy little job in sales, and she did everything they would hire her for, from typing to waitressing. Spent the rest of their time in taverns mostly. That coarsens you—spending your life in taverns. But she even managed to feel joy sometimes, along with multiple stabs of pain every single day every time she could not resist the intrusion of a random piercing memory of Kansas City. It turned out that the penance could never be paid in full. Frequent intoxication did bring temporary relief on occasion, but over time the side effects more than canceled out the benefits.

She and her mother stayed in touch a bit, a letter every once in a while telling her how the children were doing. Her father never wrote or spoke a word to her again. Clyde quickly remarried, and the new wife turned out to be a decent stepmother. A double-edged sword, that. It took away a certain kind of pain and replaced it with another kind.

She heard from the kids only once. The boy. A letter. Accusing sort of thing. Of course she didn't blame him and only thought, well, she deserved even worse. She wrote back that she was sorry and that she had loved him always and always would, and if he thought she could do anything to make up, even a little bit, for the harm she'd done them, just say the word, and she would do everything in her admittedly feeble power to accomplish it. No response to that. She shouldn't have answered him at all. That would have been better for him. His life would have been less complicated. Better that she just be the selfish monster he expected her to be, wanted her to be. Better not to have complicated his hatred, diluted his outrage.

From the girl she received not one word ever. And daughters were supposed to be so close to their mothers. But the girl had another mother to be close to, *step*mother yes, but not the one from the fairy tales, not evil at all, in fact a far worthier mother than the woman who had merely given birth to her.

And eventually she even managed to lose George. He was standing there looking out the window while she sat on the couch reading. He turned and, with great deliberation, made his way over to the couch and sat down with his most earnest look of serious purpose. She reluctantly looked up from her book, knowing this could mean nothing good, and, in an impatient tone that disguised a creeping feeling of dread, she said, "You look like you want somethin'."

"You wanna go have a drink?"

"Did you forget that we don't have any money?"

"We'll put it on the tab."

"The tab's more now than we'll ever be able ta pay. I'll be damned if I'll become a complete deadbeat in my old age."

Petulant, like a spoiled child, he rose up from the couch and returned to the window for a while but, before long, turned back to her. "Damn it, Katie. I'm goin' nuts."

"You've got cabin fever, that's all. Spring'll be here soon."

"No, it's not cabin fever. It's regret. That's what's got ahold of me. After everything, all I've got left is regret."

"You're old. That's what it's all about."

"I don't believe it. This is not what we were made for."

"Still a dreamer."

"For too damn many years I haven't even had dreams. Just trudgin' along, that's all we've been doin'. We came up here thirty-one years ago, you realize that? Thirty-one years! And haven't moved an inch in thirty-one years! Never even been to the Interior. Never even seen the Yukon River. We might as well've stayed in Kansas City."

"I wish you'd thought about that back then."

"What're you sayin'? You sayin' you wish you'd stayed there? You regret comin' with me? Then it's all been for nothin'! Nothin!"

She did not respond, which she knew would probably hurt him more than anything she could have said, but that was the way she felt.

"We stopped," he went on. "That was our mistake. We stopped. Why did we stop?"

"Where else did we have ta go? If this isn't the end of the earth, it's sure close enough. And we didn't have any more money, remember? So we had ta settle down and work. And that was it, George. The end. Just workin' and eatin' and drinkin'."

"I've been readin' and talkin' ta people. There's places up on the Yukon. Little villages. Cabins in the wilderness. Tiny little settlements. So small there isn't even an economy there. We could go up there..."

"What in the world for?"

"I don't know. Just ta do it. Just so we're not sittin' here doin' nothin'. Vegetatin', until one day we find ourselves dead."

"We'd starve. They don't even have telephones up there."

"We could get a lot of our food right from the river."

"Fish? You know what I think about fish."

"And I could hunt and trap."

"Grow up, George. You're an old man, remember?"

"I don't wanna remember. I'll leave all that sick rememberin' to you. And I'm not that old, and you're not either. All I wanna do is go on ahead and *live* the rest of my life. I wanna walk in the deep woods…"

"And get gobbled up by a bear."

"So be it. You think we're not gonna die if we stay here?"

"Maybe not so soon. Maybe not so painful either. Maybe up there we'd freeze ta death because we're too old and feeble ta go out and get more firewood. And another thing—I'm not gonna hafta use an outhouse in my old age. It's the twentieth century for God's sake."

"There'll be people up there. They ain't gonna let us freeze ta death."

"Those people didn't go up there to run a nursing home."

"I'll never go to a nursin' home. Promise me you won't ever put me in one."

"I'll put you in the nuthouse if you keep this up."

"Save your strength, I'm already there."

"Damn it, if you wanna go up in the boondocks, go on. Why do you have to try'n drag me along with you?"

"You're my wife."

"So what. I was someone else's wife once too."

"Are ya really tryin' ta punish me for that now?"

"No, George," she said with a sigh of resignation and surrender. "You're just wearin' me out here."

"If I had kids now, maybe I wouldn't feel this way."

She raised herself, sat up straighter, on high alert. "What're you sayin'?"

"I mean you claimin' to be infertile all those years when I wanted kids. I don't think that was true. You were doin' somethin' to yourself. You really think I couldn't figure that out?"

"I'll tell you what. You go right on up to the wilderness. Go anywhere except here because I don't want to live with you anymore."

"You ain't livin' at all anymore. You died years ago."

And he did leave, and she was not as unhappy to see him go as she should have been. She told herself that this time she would not be sucked in by him, would not be enticed and trapped by the dreamer and his dream. She needed to stay put and make the best of the rows she'd plowed. At the ferry dock out on Auke Bay, he held her close to him for a long time while she wished he would let her go and, on breaking away, he said tearfully, "I still love you, Katie. I'll show you it can be done, and then you can come."

She started to respond, but he shushed her. "No. Don't inflict any of your negativity on me right now. Let me have a little hope."

So she let him have his hope, and she'd be damned if he didn't seem to be doing alright, and here *she* was—old and broke in Juneau with winter coming on and only a half-wit to keep her company.

The half-wit himself was still sitting there lost in his mind, and she wanted him back with her—so she could engage with him to escape those tormenting, still-so-raw memories of a such long life of such failure. Saying something to him after so long seemed like too direct an assault so she just loudly cleared her throat, hoping that would arouse him. And, indeed, it appeared to do exactly that. He somehow found his way, or just involuntarily wandered out of, the labyrinth of his injured mind.

"What're you doin' over there?" he asked, as if *she* had been the one that had drifted away from the world rather than he.

"Nothin'. Just thinkin'."

"'Bout what?"

"Lots of things: George, my children, life, death…just run-of-the-mill crap like that."

Reuben looked around the room as if any existing children would be on the premises, then shook his head and said, "You ain't got no children."

That made her angrier than it should have. "Damn it, you know good and well that I have two grown children down in Kansas City. Your memory is getting' worse and worse."

"That crazy old George dead now?"

"Not last I heard," she said with rising impatience. "And you know that too. He's living up in the Interior, on the Yukon somewhere."

"Well, ain't he your husband?"

"Sort of. Common law."

"Then why ain't you up there with him 'stead of down here gettin' drunk in this damned old town? Huh? Why is that?"

"I just haven't wanted to," she said. "Couldn't summon up the energy. And the truth is that I've always felt like one of those boat rides would be my death warrant, just like these old tourists pouring off the cruise ships for the last trip of their lifetimes.'"

"If you don't get on that boat, you're gonna die just the same."

"That's easy enough for you to say. How old're you?"

After a long pause, he said, "I expect I'm fifty-five or so."

Scoffing, her impatience rising even more, she said, "You're not a day over forty-five, probably less—right around my son's age. You're getting worse by the day."

"Well, I'll bet you five bucks I'm still gonna die."

"Besides, it's winter up there already."

"Winter down here too. Be springtime soon enough though."

"Not for me."

"You goin' somewhere?"

She pointed down to the floor. He looked down then back up at her, puzzled.

"Into the ground," she said. "Dead."

He smiled. He could not have been happier, which pushed her all the way over the edge.

"So you think that's big fun, do you?"

"You bet. Up to the sky and be a moonbeam."

"You really believe that kind of crap, do you?"

He nodded his head vigorously. "Live in the stars!" he said, patting the little telescope hanging from his belt.

"I am so sick of damn fools. That's hokum! That's bunk! You die. You just die. Like an animal. We're animals, not angels."

"So what?"

"Dead," she said cruelly. "Forever. Nothin'. The rottenest deal of them all. All this, then nothin' at all."

"You better surrender, old woman. You better surrender!"

"To what?"

"I don't know to what. I don't care to what."

"To God maybe? Look at you. What did God ever do for you other than suck the brains right out of your head? What did God do for the Jews in the ovens? Or the babies in the dumpsters? Do ya know about that, idiot? Do ya know about that? The mothers that just throw their babies in the trash."

Very upset now, nearly weeping, wagging his head back and forth, he said, "I know you didn't do that. You didn't do that. I know you didn't."

"What? I didn't say I did it. I said it happens."

"You didn't do that to them poor babies a yours. I know you didn't."

"Well, you're wrong, Reuben, my boy. I threw them right in the trash."

"Oh no," he said. "Oh no, no, no. Got drunk and hurt them babies."

She stood up and advanced on him. "Get out! I can't stand talkin' to a moron one more minute. Get out!"

Wounded, bursting into tears, bawling like a child, he jumped up from the chair and hurried out the door.

"Goodbye, Reuben!" she yelled after him. "You won't be seein' me again."

She collapsed into the chair he had been sitting in. She felt his warmth still there and already regretted what she had done. She brought her hands to her face and sobbed. "Dreamers! God, get me rid of them!"

She wept for a while longer, and when she stopped, the very little bit of any remaining self-pity had been wrung out of her with the last of her tears. Now she had nothing and no one, not even Reuben, all brought on herself by herself, starting so long ago, back in Kansas City.

She should have done it long ago, lit herself on fire on the front lawn of what had once been her house. Or jumped out of that speeding car along that Kansas highway. A few bounces and scrapes and it would have been over. It wouldn't have been enough, but it would be all she could do to expiate her sin. For that's what it was, old-fashioned sin, about as mortal of a sin as you could inflict on your children short of physically torturing or killing them. Why did she think she could escape it? The misery she had caused herself all these years—and caused George, and maybe a few others too, even poor Reuben today—by prolonging her useless, outcast existence. She had kept on through those first years in Juneau only in hopes that somehow something would save her, show her a way out of the trap she had made for herself, provide her some miraculous way to make things right.

Never happened. Couldn't happen. Wouldn't ever happen. It had all gotten beyond her a long time ago, maybe from the beginning, when she had fled Kansas City to Juneau, so close to near the very end of the earth, instead of staying there at home and facing the music for the rest of her life if that's what it took. George and his damn Alaska dream! But he had been right in that diner back in Kansas. She had just hopped onto his shabby little dented up boxcar of a dream so she would not have to face what she had done—day after day, all day and night, and all the days of the year there in Kansas City where there was neither nook nor cranny in which to take even a moment's refuge.

"All right, Rueben," she said out loud. "I surrender. I don't want anything anymore—nothing but nothing."

She found herself in the kitchen looking down at the stove. She had long thought this would be the simplest, easiest way. 'No fuss, no muss', as they say. Years and years ago she had read something that had stayed with her and sat heavy on her mind right now—about that poet woman in England who had left her kids with a friend and then put her head in the oven and left her own life. It seemed like the perfect way really.

Despite her fantasies of lighting herself on fire in her front yard, burning at the stake like one of the witches of old Salem, she knew she could not bear the agony of death by fire. Just ending it was enough, it did not have to be horrifying.

So now she made sure the pilot light was off and turned the gas up high, hoping the kitchen was not too drafty. She opened the oven door, which folded out, furnishing a useful flat shelf on which she intended to rest her head. She slid the grills out and set them down on the floor away from the front of the stove. She would need to sit or kneel on the floor. That would be rough. The arthritis in her knees, the hard tile floor, the uncomfortable metal of the oven door. Pillows. There were pillows in the bedroom. But it seemed like such a long way there and back. She feared she would falter on that long round-trip. But she managed it without misadventure and grimly congratulated herself as she arrived back in front of the stove with two pillows. She placed one pillow on the floor and the other on the shelf made by the open oven door, and arranged herself on the floor, overcoming the arthritic pain in her knees as she worked herself into a tolerable position. She crossed her arms on top of the pillow on the open oven door, turned her head to the side, and positioned it as close to the oven interior as she could. It was not very comfortable despite the pillows. It turned out that killing herself was not going to be all that much easier than anything else in life had been. But maybe with just a little more discomfort it would all be over. Although the last thirty-one years of her life had almost all seemed like a penance, it had not been enough, yet this small final payment on her hopelessly large and long overdue penitential account would have to do.

She inhaled as deeply as she could, but nausea from the gas smell made her want to vomit, and she had to quickly switch to a shallower breathing. She wondered if she would be able to go through with it. Cowardice again. *Gone forever.* The thought of that. It seemed impossible. And especially to choose it voluntarily, all hope lost. She needed help. A sleeping pill or two would've come in handy. But she didn't have any. If she could, just this once, calm her racing, jumping, bitter, self-hating thoughts...

Remember you have no reason to stay. Not for a long, long time have you had any reason.

No reason...

No reason...

No reason...

She had finally found the way. She kept silently reciting "no reason" until it became a soothing mantra for dying. She thought she might even be able to drift off to sleep—if she could just keep breathing, handle the smell without gagging.

No reason...no reason...no reason...

"What you doin'? It stinks in here."

For a moment she didn't understand. The sudden wholly unexpected presence of another person in the room frightened her. She emitted something between a grunt and a scream and lifted her head to see Reuben standing there with a newly bought coffee can in his hand. He set it on the stove as he reached over and turned off the gas.

"Crazy woman, you a damn fool or what? You could kill your old self."

"What the hell. I told ya ta get out. Go! Leave me alone."

"I ain't goin' nowhere. I decided to forgive you, old girl. Even for them babies. Everything's okay now. Time for coffee now. And fried fish for dinner."

Looking up at him, she thought, well, that's it. It isn't gonna happen. Not now anyway. Like it or not, this misbegotten little creature had just saved her life, damn him to hell. She pulled herself up from the floor, slid the pillow off the oven door, and slammed the door shut. With the pillow in one hand, she impulsively grabbed him in a rough embrace. He didn't really seem to understand what she was doing or why, but he did seem to understand that it was some sort of gesture of goodwill and submitted to it until she let him go.

She stared at him, tears streaming down her face, but she was also smiling. Seeming embarrassed by her crying and smiling and hugging, he stuffed his hands in the pockets of his coat. A puzzled look came over him, and he pulled something out of his pocket. An envelope.

"What's this?" he said, looking down at it, trying to remember. "It's for you. Hey, Katie! I found somethin' for you in your mailbox. Been there all this day long."

He handed her the envelope. She opened it and took out a folded-up letter. Something inserted in the letter fell out onto the floor. She bent down, picked it up, looked at it, and laughed.

"What's so funny?" he said.

She barked a little laugh. "A ferry ticket."

"Uh-oh. You gonna die now sure thing."

"Shh! Let me read this. Get some coffee ready to boil. Can you do the pilot light without blowing us up?"

She moved to the kitchen table, sat down, and read the letter.

Dear Katie:

I probably just went and squandered my money because I don't suppose you'll ever really use this ticket. But I've still got some faith, so here's hoping. I won't tell you any lies. It's not super easy up here, especially in the winter, and winter's coming on. We already had our first snowfall. A light one, but snow it was. But I managed to shoot a moose last month so I've got some meat. And I found a good place to saw a hole in the ice so I can fish this winter. Yes, I know you don't like fish. I'll eat the fish, you eat the meat. And remember, we've got our Social Security. And I'm not saying it doesn't get real lonely sometimes and way too cold. But there's moments that are worth living for (and dying for too), I'll tell you that. Nothing real spectacular, but the other day I managed to climb up to a high place above the river just after dawn. I stayed there all morning. Nothing much to see—a bear and her cubs walking along the water. And then down the river, straight down the middle of it, comes soaring along—a falcon—a peregrine falcon. They don't live much of any place in the world anymore except here. And when he went on his way, it was just me and the trees and the river then. And I thought, "I'm ready to die now. I really am. Right here. Right now." And I thought about just staying up there watching until I froze or starved to death. And the snow would just come on and cover me up.

But I came back to the cabin. I'm not ready to go yet. Too damn scared. Maybe I'll never be ready, but it seems to be getting better all the time. Come, Katie. All you've got there is your regrets. And if you die on the ferry like you're crazily afraid that you might, that's as good of a place as any to go, floating on down the Inside Passage in the middle of a world only God could have made. Come. Please come. Choose life, Katie, just one more time.

She set the letter down on the table and looked up at nothing in particular. It had probably arrived yesterday—been there yesterday and all day today—in the mailbox and in Reuben's pocket while her head was in the oven.

"I'll be damned," she said.

THEY SAT IN silence in the back seat of the taxi. Katie just watched Reuben as he stared ahead, lost in his mind again. She reached over and rested her hand lightly on his shoulder. His trance broken, he looked around, confused. For a moment she thought he might even have forgotten who she was.

"It's night," he said.

"Early morning," she said. "It will be dawn before long."

"I forgot where we're goin'."

"Auke Bay. Where the ferry is."

"Am I goin' somewhere?"

"No. Not today anyway. But I am, remember?"

He looked around a little wildly—in front, to the side, then back. "How'm I gettin' back home?"

"The driver'll be taking you back."

Reuben just shrugged. She thought he might be falling right back into the trance, but he nodded his head very seriously, then looked at her. "I know you've got to go up there ta...—"

She did not fill in the blank. She had learned that was not helpful, unless he definitively came up empty after a suitable period of deliberation.

"George!" Reuben finally said, excited and proud. "George. Right?"

"Right as rain." She looked out the window and thought how it would soon start raining, seemingly day after day, for a long time.

"But no kids up there, right?" he burst out again.

"No, not up there."

"Up on the Yukon!" he said joyfully, delighted that he had remembered yet one more thing.

"Yes."

"You're a real pioneer, Katie."

"I guess so," she said ruefully.

At the ferry station the cars were lined up in several long rows. The attendants loitered around, hands in their pockets to keep them warm, waiting for the signal to start loading. The "footsies,"—the foot passengers—were lined up behind a thin rope. The taxi stopped. She sat there, not moving, in a bit of a trance..

"We're here, lady," the taxi driver said. When she did not respond, he said, louder, "Hey, lady. We're here."

She fished some bills out of her jacket pocket and leaned forward to pay him. "You wait here, alright? He'll only be a few minutes, and then you take him back right where you picked him up. Don't let him tell you ta drop him off anywhere else. Take him right back ta where ya got him."

"Somethin' wrong with that fella?" the taxi driver asked in a low, conspiratorial voice, looking suspiciously in his rearview mirror. "He off his rocker or somethin'?"

"No. He just gets lost a little easier'n the rest of us, that's all. Come on, Reuben."

On the dock they stood looking up at the big boat.

"You not afraid a that little old damned boat, are ya, Katie? You not afraid a that, are ya?"

"I'm scared to death of it."

He laughed merrily.

"What're ya gonna do without me ta take care of?" she said.

He just grinned.

"What's gonna happen to ya, Reuben?" she said, more to herself than to him. "What's gonna happen?"

"What you doin'? Cryin' now? I swear I never seen you cry before no how. You that scared a that little old damned boat? Huh?"

She grabbed him and hugged him.

"Better get on there," he said. "No cold feet now. Not now."

"I'll write you letters."

"Can't read much no more."

"I'll write 'em anyway."

"No drinkin'. Don't be forgettin' about that."

"Goodbye, Reuben."

Beatific, she thought. That was the word for his smile. *May you smile that way forever, Reuben.*

She walked down the ramp with her small suitcase in one hand, her purse in another, leaning forward from the heavy pack strapped to her back. She stopped and looked back. He grinned and waved enthusiastically. She took her place in line and vowed not to look back again. Here she was again. The last time she had boarded a ferry was thirty-one years ago. Following George then. Following George again now.

After a little while, she couldn't help herself, she looked back. Reuben stood on the dock with his telescope trained on what remained of the night sky. The cab driver came up to him, took his arm, and pointed back toward the cab. Reuben tugged backward a little, apparently not understanding what was happening, seemingly thinking—who is this person pulling on me and making me go somewhere I don't know? She was afraid the cab driver might just give up on him. But then Reuben relented and let himself be led away.

Ensconced back in the cab, the driver looked suspiciously in the rearview mirror again, checking on his confused but compliant passenger, and began backing up. Just as the driver completed his backward maneuver, turned around, switched from reverse to drive, now ready to accelerate forward and return to the city, the back door opened, and she piled into the back seat—backpack, suitcase, and all—forcing Reuben to skootch over to accommodate her and her belongings.

"Hey," Reuben said, "what's goin' on?"

"We're goin' fishin'," she said. "Winter'll be here before ya can say 'Jack Robinson.'"

"Can't say as I know him."